The place seemed completely deserted

Suddenly there was a buzzing sound as a door in the bank of elevators down the hallway opened. A group of men and women walked out and casually strolled toward the front entrance.

The Executioner froze. People were still in the building.

Either Taylor hadn't been able to evacuate the place or she hadn't understood his cryptic message at the meet. In any case, it meant Bolan was out of options.

But the sudden sound of an alarm changed everything in a split second. Bolan heard shouts coming from the front of the building. A moment later, Taylor rounded a corner with a gun in hand. The crazy MI-6 agent charged the trio, leveling the muzzle of her weapon and screaming something at the top of her lungs.

The Executioner reached inside his coveralls for the Beretta 93-R as the madwoman opened fire.

MACK BOLAN®
The Executioner

#208 Death Whisper
#209 Asian Crucible
#210 Fire Lash
#211 Steel Claws
#212 Ride the Beast
#213 Blood Harvest
#214 Fission Fury
#215 Fire Hammer
#216 Death Force
#217 Fight or Die
#218 End Game
#219 Terror Intent
#220 Tiger Stalk
#221 Blood and Fire
#222 Patriot Gambit
#223 Hour of Conflict
#224 Call to Arms
#225 Body Armor
#226 Red Horse
#227 Blood Circle
#228 Terminal Option
#229 Zero Tolerance
#230 Deep Attack
#231 Slaughter Squad
#232 Jackal Hunt
#233 Tough Justice
#234 Target Command
#235 Plague Wind
#236 Vengeance Rising
#237 Hellfire Trigger
#238 Crimson Tide
#239 Hostile Proximity
#240 Devil's Guard
#241 Evil Reborn
#242 Doomsday Conspiracy
#243 Assault Reflex
#244 Judas Kill
#245 Virtual Destruction
#246 Blood of the Earth
#247 Black Dawn Rising
#248 Rolling Death
#249 Shadow Target
#250 Warning Shot
#251 Kill Radius
#252 Death Line
#253 Risk Factor
#254 Chill Effect
#255 War Bird
#256 Point of Impact
#257 Precision Play
#258 Target Lock
#259 Nightfire
#260 Dayhunt
#261 Dawnkill
#262 Trigger Point
#263 Skysniper
#264 Iron Fist
#265 Freedom Force
#266 Ultimate Price
#267 Invisible Invader
#268 Shattered Trust
#269 Shifting Shadows
#270 Judgment Day
#271 Cyberhunt
#272 Stealth Striker
#273 UForce
#274 Rogue Target
#275 Crossed Borders
#276 Leviathan
#277 Dirty Mission
#278 Triple Reverse
#279 Fire Wind
#280 Fear Rally
#281 Blood Stone
#282 Jungle Conflict
#283 Ring of Retaliation

DON PENDLETON'S

THE EXECUTIONER®

RING OF RETALIATION

A GOLD EAGLE BOOK FROM

WORLDWIDE®

TORONTO • NEW YORK • LONDON
AMSTERDAM • PARIS • SYDNEY • HAMBURG
STOCKHOLM • ATHENS • TOKYO • MILAN
MADRID • WARSAW • BUDAPEST • AUCKLAND

First edition June 2002
ISBN 0-373-64283-0

Special thanks and acknowledgment to
Jon Guenther for his contribution to this work.

RING OF RETALIATION

Printed in U.S.A.

Ancient of days! august Athena! where,
Where are thy men of might? thy grand in soul?
Gone—glimmering through the dream of things
that were.

—Lord Byron (1788–1824)

While the dreams of heroes and mighty men might be lost, the innocent should take heart. Because I won't ever abandon anyone to the evil devices of terrorism.

—Mack Bolan

For Steve Mertz—
an old pro who encouraged a new one

Prologue

Thessaloníki, Greece

The 107 mm HE submunitions bomb exploded approximately three hundred meters above the street in an orange flash.

A score of security men for the Honorable Audrey Hyde-Baker burst from their places near the motorcade and began a coordinated effort to secure the area, which left a skeleton crew to protect Hyde-Baker as they fanned out and studied the roofs above them.

Trying to protect someone in that situation wasn't ideal, but Hyde-Baker had refused to listen to her protectors. She didn't care what they thought. Her mission to Greece was important, and that took precedence over security. She refused to be intimidated by those cretins calling themselves revolutionaries. And if she died as a result of her beliefs, so be it. Perhaps it would lead to more aggressive reprisal by Greek officials.

With only a few days to the arrival of the rest of the NATO delegates, Hyde-Baker wanted to establish a working relationship with the citizenry that was based upon trust and admiration. Surely the people of Greece were getting as tired of the violence in their country as the rest of the world. No amount of threats or intimidation could oppose the idealism of a new Greece that was free from terrorism.

Hyde-Baker believed in that cause, and she was willing to show the people of Greece that her actions spoke as loud as her words.

She risked a glance out her window and up to the sky where the last of the fiery blast had dissipated. It didn't appear that there was any danger at all. The blast was actually behind her vehicle, and so it couldn't have caused harm to her anyway. Someone was just trying to make a statement. Perhaps it was just a bloody firework intended to say "Welcome," perhaps a warning. In either case, it didn't seem to be much of a threat.

Hyde-Baker sat back in her seat and relaxed.

CYRIL HELONAS SMILED as he watched the security team for the Hyde-Baker bitch spread out.

It would only be a matter of seconds before his plan saw its awakening. Within the hour, the British ambassador would be under his control. Then he would announce her capture to her country. Their demands would be met—the British thought too much of themselves and their people to let one die needlessly.

Hyde-Baker was foolish anyway, allowing herself to be caught in such a predicament. All of her flamboyance and gallantry would be gone in the next minute. Their plan was so obvious that it defied logic, just like when two brave souls from their group had taken out Saunders a few years before. It seemed like a lifetime since that job. But then how could one put a timeline on revolution?

In any case, the time to act had come. And it did so in a very dramatic way.

Inside the GRM20 bomb—which had been fired from a 4.2-inch mortar positioned carefully atop the Respires Towers—were twenty M-20 G minibombs. They were simple cylinders that deployed a shaped charge by parachute. They were small, hardly visible to the naked eye until they were practically on top of the target—especially on such a gray and cloudy day like this one.

Helonas watched through the glass of the coffee shop as, true to his prediction, the minibombs deployed on target and detonated at impact. Hundreds of lethal fragments saturated an area of almost seven thousand square meters.

In the center of that carnage was a busload of unwary tourists, including seventeen women and about two dozen children. The thin metal of the bus couldn't withstand the force of those multiple blasts. Sharp, jagged pellets tore through the interior as the bombs exploded on and around the vehicle. Superheated metal and glass punctured vital organs or ripped flesh from the tourists.

Screams began to emanate from the crowd, and the entire block erupted into pandemonium.

The British and Greek security agents responded just as Helonas had predicted, rushing toward the crowd to render whatever assistance they could. That left only four agents for Hyde-Baker—inadequate protection against their people. Helonas left the shop and moved into position, heading directly toward the vehicle. The security agents surrounding Hyde-Baker's car were still fixated on devastation to their rear, intent on believing that any threat to the ambassador would come from that direction.

It was a fatal mistake.

Helonas and five other members of the group converged simultaneously on Hyde-Baker's Mercedes. They produced Zastava M-85 SMGs from beneath their coats and opened fire. The weapons could have been mistaken for Russian-made AKSU-74s, except that these were Yugoslavian weapons and favored the 5.56 mm cartridges over the 5.45 mm in the AKSU.

Helonas's first hit scored on one of the rear guards. Slugs from the M-85 punched through the British agent's chest before blowing bits of his spine out the other end. The man's finger curled reflexively around the trigger of his Spectre subgun and sent a few rounds into the sky before he was slammed against the Mercedes. He slid to the street, leaving a gory streak on the vehicle.

The sheer terror and chaos in the street behind Hyde-Baker's car had created a complete gridlock in the traffic flow. Nobody could go anywhere. Some of the citizens were actually jumping from their vehicles while others searched for an escape route. There was no place for the Mercedes driver to go, in any case, and that fact cost him his life.

As the other members in Helonas's group dispatched the remaining guards in similar fashion, the terrorist opened up the front door and shot the unarmed driver in the head at point-blank range. The heavy-caliber slug blew his brains across the front seat. Helonas gestured for one of his men to take the wheel as he dragged the nearly headless corpse from the sedan.

Police were now approaching the area, and the terrorist group had taken up positions as security. They ripped off their outer garments to reveal pressed suits. They gestured to arriving police units that they needed to get Hyde-Baker to safety.

"There's some trouble back there," Helonas told one of the officers. "Several of our people have gone to help, but we need to clear this street."

The rush of people and the slow crawl in traffic aptly covered the bodies of the dead agents from view. The Greek law officers began to disperse the motorized traffic to allow for a clean escape. Helonas smiled with grim satisfaction as he jumped into the back seat of the Mercedes.

Audrey Hyde-Baker stared back at the Greek terrorist with a mixture of fear and resentment. Her normally haughty mask wasn't there. She had finally witnessed the effectiveness of the organization firsthand. There was little left to her resolve now, which was all the better as far as Helonas was concerned. It would make it easier to break her.

She reached for the door, but Helonas grabbed her by her silvery strands of hair and put the hot muzzle of the Zastava M-85 under her chin. The wig came off in his hand, and he grunted with surprise as Hyde-Baker grabbed for his crotch. He blocked the move and seized her throat. Their struggle wasn't visible to the outside—thanks to the tinted windows—and Helonas gritted his teeth as he closed his hand around Hyde-Baker's throat.

She tried to let out a squeal of outrage, but it was choked off by the steellike tendons that blocked the air from her lungs and blood from her brain. Helonas tightened his fingers even more, and fought to restrain himself from killing the woman there and then. He hated this British whore for all she had done to discredit his people. Helonas finally let go and watched with amusement as Hyde-Baker wheezed for air.

"You have no idea how much I will enjoy watching you die, Madam Secretary," Helonas said with the frostiest smile he could manage. "How much all of us will enjoy watching you die."

"Go to bloody hell, you baby-killing monster," Hyde-Baker managed through her gasps.

"I already am in hell," Helonas replied. "And now you have joined me."

Stony Man Farm, Virginia

"They call themselves the Revolutionary Organization 17 November," Hal Brognola announced. "And they're dangerous."

"It sounded on the phone as if this mission was special," the Executioner replied.

Mack Bolan sat across from Brognola in the War Room. Barbara Price sat with them, but to this point she had remained silent. Something had been troubling her since Bolan's arrival, but he saw no point in questioning her about it. That wasn't his place—he knew it and so did she. Not that Price would have minded his asking, or even kept personal information from him if he had.

That just wasn't the nature of their relationship. Basically, it didn't work that way because it couldn't work that way. If things got too personal between them, they knew it could spell trouble in the long run. Price would end up pining away for her man at the Farm, and Bolan might afford a distraction that would snowball into a fatal misstep during a mission. It was better this way.

"This one is special, Striker," Brognola replied quietly.

"I'm familiar with 17 November's activities. Didn't they take credit for the murder of Brigadier Saunders?"

"Yes," Brognola confirmed, a trace of bitterness in his voice. "Stephen was an acquaintance. At the time he was serving in Athens as the British military attaché. Two gunmen on a motorcycle pulled up next to his car while he was on his way to work, pointed a pistol at him and fired four shots." The anger in Brognola's voice cracked a little as he added, "He died of complications from chest and belly wounds a couple hours later."

"What was the motive?"

"They claimed he had a major role in NATO's air strikes against Yugoslavia in 1999. The British Ministry of Defence adamantly denied any role in that, a position they stand by to this day."

"What makes this most recent attack so odd," Price said, breaking her silence, "was that a significant number of Greek citizens were either injured or killed by the mortar bomb they launched over the street."

"Mortar bomb?" the soldier echoed.

"Police said it was a GRM20," Brognola interjected helpfully. "Greek designed and manufactured."

Bolan nodded. "Yeah, it's a nasty little device. I've seen it in action now and again. Very popular among terrorists because of its wide-range effects. That makes it the perfect weapon for urban assault."

"Despite the oddities," Price continued, "this operation falls well inside the scope of 17 November's aims. In the past four years, they've been implicated in or directly credited for at least fifty attacks. That's three times the number they were involved in during the seventies and eighties. Their targets have always been diplomats, and it didn't change with this operation."

"Actually, the attack was a diversion, Striker," Brognola said. "They got everybody's attention away from the real goal."

"Which was?" Bolan prompted.

"The kidnapping of Audrey Hyde-Baker," Price replied with a sigh, "the undersecretary for the Foreign and Commonwealth Office of Great Britain."

"She's been instrumental in coordinating this meeting between the NATO subcommittee and officials of the Greek government," Brognola added.

"The Sheringham Articles," Bolan said with a nod.

"That's right," Price replied. "The NATO Anti-Terrorism Committee has put together an impressive package for the Greek Foreign Ministry. It's a comprehensive list of suggested changes to Greek law, along with a promise of financial aid from the U.S. and England."

"The assassination of Stephen Saunders was a turning point in relations between Greece and the United States," Brognola said. "Law enforcement got aggressive in trying to locate the members of 17 November responsible for Saunders's death, but their efforts were futile and the excitement died down. That was when Hyde-Baker stepped in and pushed for the formation of the NATO group."

"Sounds like some of the finest minds were put to the test on this one," Bolan remarked.

"You're not kidding there," Price agreed, pulling a sheet of paper from a file folder. "The official proposal won't be released until the end of the week, but Aaron used our clearance to pull what we could. Some of the changes include amnesty for group members who agree to give up their fellow members, creation of a special court to prosecute terrorists and rewards and protection for witnesses." Price replaced the paper and slid the folder across the table.

"They're not wasting any time," Bolan said. He shook his head on afterthought, adding, "But we all know that you can't reason with terrorists. Written measures, no matter how decent the intent, can't replace decisive action."

"I would agree," Brognola replied. "That's why we asked you here."

"I understand," the Executioner said in a noncommittal fashion.

He knew his tone of voice had solicited the knowing smile that played across the Stony Man chief's lips. The Executioner ran his own agenda and he kept the lines of communication with his government narrow—very narrow. Only Brognola and the other members within the Stony Man organization could command his attention. They never burdened the Executioner with a problem. If Brognola called on him, the warrior knew it was important enough for him to listen.

"The kidnapping of Hyde-Baker aside," Brognola said, "there's a growing concern that the conference is in danger."

"What conference?"

"Five days from now, the NATO subcommittee will meet in Athens with the Greek foreign minister, public order minister, new democracy deputy and justice minister."

"And that's just for starters," Price added.

Bolan whistled. "Those are some heavy hitters."

"There's also a promise of increased cooperation between British and Greek law-enforcement officers. As a matter of fact, the SAS has agreed to set up an academy to assist Greek police officers in counterterrorist techniques."

"That's a step in the right direction," Bolan stated.

"But it's still a long way off," Brognola told him. "And it won't happen if this conference doesn't have positive results."

"I take it that's where I come in."

"Absolutely," Price replied. "In that file is information on a woman named Dina Taylor. She's a special operative with MI-6, and she's been inside Athens on a covert op for some time. She's made contacts in their underground, and she thinks she's linked up with a member of the Anti-State Action."

"Who are they?"

"We think that's just a front name for 17 November."

"Sounds weak," Bolan countered.

"Maybe," Price offered, "but the British government's taking it seriously and so are we. If she is close to 17 November, it will be the first time anyone's ever penetrated the group."

"Imagine an organization," Brognola interjected, "that nobody seems to really know anything about. Not one member of this group has ever been arrested or detained, let alone positively identified. We're convinced of two things. One, they decide on their targets as a whole. No one individual is in charge, and no freelancing is permitted. Two, they're a very small group with probably thirty members or less."

Bolan nodded. "That would explain why it's been so hard to identify anyone within the organization."

"That was our assessment, as well," Brognola replied. "The other point here is that they are now threatening to kill Hyde-Baker if the British government doesn't call off the conference."

"Why hasn't any of this has been in the papers?" Bolan queried.

It was Price who answered. "Because the demands were made directly to the prime minister, and only top-ranking members knew Hyde-Baker was scheduled to arrive in Greece early by way of Thessaloníki. Plus, the meeting in Athens wasn't scheduled to be announced until the day it took place."

"Not giving anyone time to retaliate," the Executioner concluded.

"Probably."

The soldier looked at Brognola. "Any idea how they knew Hyde-Baker was going to be in Greece?"

"No," Brognola said, shoving an unlit cigar in his mouth and shaking his head. "And that's one of the things that bothers me. We're thinking it was a leak somewhere in their security teams, but there's really no proof."

Bolan opened the file folder and went to the section on Dina Taylor. "What about this agent they have here. Any chance she mentioned it to the source she's into?"

"There's always that chance," Price replied, "but we're pretty certain she didn't talk to anyone."

"Did she know about it?"

"Yes."

"Then she's a risk," Bolan growled.

"We don't think so. Taylor's got quite an impressive record. She trained with the same SAS unit as McCarter. She has one of the most impeccable records in British service. She even holds a degree from Oxford. She transferred to MI-6 about four years ago. My intelligence sources tell me that Taylor has a reputation as one of the best in the espionage game."

"Yeah, but even a professional can get sloppy," Bolan reminded her. "They can let their guard down and before they realize it, it's too late. Especially with a group as clever as 17 November."

"We have to consider the possibility that the security leak came right from someone within the Greek government," Brognola postulated.

It was obvious the Greeks hadn't learned their lesson. The file listed sketchy details about the attacks to which Price had alluded earlier. There was every indication that 17 November was well equipped and informed. Almost every target in their history had some sort of diplomatic undertone. Within the past five years, they had utilized rockets, bombs and small arms to attack visiting dignitaries and prominent businesspeople.

Bolan knew their motives were centered on an anticapitalist, antiimperialist view. They strongly discouraged the presence of U.S. or NATO military bases in Greece, and they were highly critical of the Greek government over such things as current affairs in Cyprus. Their name was derived from a student uprising in Athens that took place in the early 1970s. A military-run Greece had eventually put down the coup at that time. Again, the poor response of the Greek government had resulted in the birth of one of the most evasive and mysterious terrorist groups in the world.

Present policies were ineffective in quelling this new outbreak of boldness by 17 November and its members. The kidnapping of Undersecretary Hyde-Baker could result in strained relations between Greece and her allies. It could have a particularly profound effect on U.S. aid to Greece, since it was no secret that Congress strongly criticized Greek apathy to this date.

For an organization like 17 November to operate that long without a single arrest or surgical strike was ridiculous at best. It told Bolan several things about the Greek government, not the least of which was evidence of strong political ties between elected officials and members of 17 November.

The whole thing smelled of trouble to the Executioner's way of thinking.

"So what's the angle?" Bolan finally asked.

"We want to use this Taylor's connection to get you inside the organization," Brognola pitched. "If there's any chance we are dealing with 17 November, then you're the most qualified person to break down the walls."

"And once I'm inside?"

"That will be left completely up to you." Brognola cleared his throat, looked at Price and then added, "We're pretty certain that they'll make good on their threat to murder the undersecretary. Taylor's in place to assist you in getting her out."

"No dice, Hal," the Executioner cut in. "You know my policy. I work alone."

"I told the Man you would say that but—"

"He's still asking," Bolan finished.

"This hasn't exactly been sanctioned by the President," Price explained. "He's doing this at the request of Her Majesty via the prime minister."

"This is a request from the queen of England?" Bolan asked.

"And others," Brognola said with a shrug. "In either case, it's coming from the highest levels. The Royal Family knows that the measures in this conference are just as important to U.S. interests as they are to those of the British. Not only has 17 November operated against its own government, which is coincidentally the most recent member of the European Common Market, but also against British involvement in Turkey and U.S. interests in the Balkans."

"There's another side to this story, though," Price said, "and this could be the most intriguing part of it all."

"What's that?"

"Well, have you ever heard of a man named Kermit Albertson?"

Bolan had to think back, flipping through his mental files before he came up with a face to match a name. Over the years, he'd perfected his memory and it was nearly photographic. It might have paled in comparison to that of Aaron "The Bear"

Kurtzman's steel trap, but it was still effective enough to serve the Executioner when it counted most.

"Yeah," he murmured after a moment. "Deputy director of CIA operations in the independent-states regions."

"Right again," Price said in an even tone.

"What part does he play in this?"

"He can point the finger at major members within the government who have ties to these revolutionaries. He was privy to some very sensitive information, and he rubbed elbows with everything from brass in law enforcement right on up to members of the Foreign and Commonwealth Office. He's scheduled to appear at the meeting and spill his guts, as well."

"That's something they're keeping under tight wraps," Brognola added. "I had to practically pry that information out of the Man himself."

"So that leaves little doubt another attack by 17 November could be disastrous," Bolan admitted. "I'm just curious to know who inside the British government stands to gain if they do come through on their threats."

"It could be someone from the British Parliamentary Foreign Affairs Committee," Price suggested.

"How so, Barb?" Brognola asked.

"They've repeatedly accused the FCO of not doing enough to protect British dignitaries within Greece, and they use some pretty strong language every time they do so."

Brognola shook his head with disgust. "Politics."

"Again," the Executioner added, "and it doesn't surprise me in the least. I guess the bottom line is I accept the mission, and this Taylor is the string, or I can walk away."

"Yes," Brognola replied hollowly, "you can walk away."

"They're saying take it or leave it, Mack," Price said quietly. "We know how you feel about that."

"Yeah." Bolan grimaced and tossed the file on the table. "But there's too much at stake to turn it down." He looked at the big Fed and continued, "So I guess you can count me in, Hal."

"I was hoping you'd say that."

"What's the plan?"

"I'll let Barb brief you on that," Brognola said, rising from his chair. "I hate to run, but I have an appointment in Wonderland in less than an hour. Jack's waiting for me."

"I guess I'll see you when I get back, then."

Brognola nodded, shook the Executioner's hand and then headed for the door. Just as he reached the exit, he turned to look at Bolan.

"Hey, Striker?"

"Yeah?"

"Watch your ass on this one. I smell trouble."

"Bet on it," Bolan replied.

When Brognola was gone, the Executioner fixed Price with a longing stare. It was good to see her again. Hell, it was good to see all of them again. He actually spent quite a bit of time at the Farm, but it never seemed like enough. The members of Stony Man were family—the only real family he had, save for Johnny. But even his kid brother rarely got into the picture.

Johnny had his own life now, and his own interests to pursue. Bolan couldn't blame him. He just wasn't cut out for the same road as the Executioner. This fateful destiny was handed to an elect few, and the soldier was glad that at least one man with the last name of Bolan didn't have to walk one bloody mile after another in the War Everlasting. Still, it troubled him at times.

"Where you at, Mack?" Price asked.

"Just thinking about something," Bolan said. "So, what's the plan here?"

Price got back to business. "You'll be posing as a tactician, cover name of Michalis Belapoulos."

"Clever," Bolan quipped. "Sounds very Greek."

"Thanks," Price shot back with a grin. "I picked it myself."

"I'll bet."

"You're a Greek national, been out of the country in an Argentine prison for the past eight years. Your specialty is small arms and tactics." She removed a picture from the file and pointed to a muscular man with a dark complexion. He appeared to be talking to a strikingly beautiful woman with blond hair. "This man will be your contact. We know him only as Midas."

"Who's the woman?"

"That's Dina Taylor. This picture was taken by one of her fellow agents. We think it's the first time any member of 17 November has been photographed, so memorize that face."

"Done. When do I leave?"

"There's a direct flight out of Dulles. We'll send Jack ahead when he's finished here, just in case you need him."

"Well, then, I'd better get packed," Bolan said. "I've got a plane to catch."

Athens, Greece

Greek music resounded from speakers throughout the club. The acrid stench of cigarette smoke and ouzo hung in the air.

Dina Taylor didn't really pay attention to it as she sat in a booth and waited for her contact. Things with Midas were becoming a bit too serious; she was beginning to sense his growing attraction to her. That bothered Taylor in a lot of respects, although this wasn't the first time for this kind of thing. Men were always attracted to her for some strange reason.

She'd never considered herself a raving beauty, but most of those in the male species would have strongly disagreed. She had a nice body—fine-tuned by two hours a day in one of the local gyms and continuous practice in martial arts—but she figured there were a lot of women in the same shape. Maybe it had something to do with that male ego that just wouldn't let some men date anything less than a supermodel.

Then again, there was her job. She'd sacrificed a lot for her government, and Britain wasn't an easy boss to work for. Taylor had completely given up on the idea of ever having children or a husband. As a member of MI-6, anything resembling a "normal" life was out of the question. Oh, sure, a lot of agents in the intelligence agency had families, but they also had years of field experience and now many of them were pushing a desk. Taylor could have a family, too, if she wanted to give up the field.

But at the moment, it was more important for her to be out here. She needed her independence. She wasn't ready to settle down, and even if she were, it wouldn't have been with the likes of Midas. There was something just slimy about the guy, something reptilian. Not to mention the fact he was probably a member of one of the most violent terrorist groups on the face of the whole bloody planet.

And speak of the devil, Taylor noticed Midas walk through the front door of the club. She let him look around for almost a minute before finally signaling for his attention. Let the little twit wait awhile.

But also a dangerous twit, she reminded herself.

Midas made his way through the club and sat across from her, his black eyes glittering like coals in the dim lights. He kept his head shaved, and it was lighter than his dark skin. The guy needed to get more sun to allow uniform color, but when he was outside he kept a leather cap on his head. Taylor could barely see the line of the cap in the low-level lights, but it was ever present and it drove her bats.

"Hello, Flower," Midas said, grabbing her hand and kissing it before she could stop him.

Probably the closest contact with the opposite sex he's had in a year, Taylor mused. "You're late," she said.

"I know, I know," he said, shrugging out of his coat. "I had some last-minute business that needed my attention. I could not get out of the office."

Taylor knew it was a lie, but she made no attempt to confront him with it. Midas worked as a city journalist for Pontiki, a local newspaper of some popularity in Athens. He didn't really need the money, since he was the only nephew of Deputy Justice Minister Amphionides, who was charged with the administration of internal security. Amphionides and his entire family had been financially independent prior to his appointment to the justice ministry. Now, they were even more well-to-do in society.

Given Midas's connections with the Greek government and his admitted involvement with Anti-State Action, Taylor wondered if it was Midas who had told 17 November of Undersecretary Hyde-Baker's visit to Thessaloníki. It wouldn't only explain how they knew, but it would go a long way toward proving collusion between the terrorist group and the government. It would also explain why in over twenty-five years of terrorist actions there had never been one arrest of a 17 November criminal.

The murder of Brigadier Stephen Saunders had created a tidal wave of outrage in London. Saunders had been a longtime family friend of the Taylors. In some respects, Taylor felt she'd dedicated herself to bringing down 17 November as much for the sake of that friendship as for the safe return of Hyde-Baker.

And now, here sat the one person who could probably facilitate that act. She couldn't blow it, especially since she'd been informed early that morning of the impending arrival of the American agent.

"I have some good news for you," Midas said, intruding on her thoughts as if he'd been reading them like an open book.

Taylor did her best to put on a sweet smile for him and not pull her hand away. "And what's that?"

"Well, I talked to my friend," Midas began slowly. He had to pause to give his drink order and continued after the waitress walked away. "You know...my friend. The one we talked about before."

"Really?" Taylor retorted with mock excitement. She let out a giggle. "Oh, what did he say, Midas?"

Midas paused a moment and raised his eyebrows. He wrinkled his nose to increase the anticipation and Taylor waited, watching him intently as he tried to build the tension. All she could think of was how weak and ugly he was.

"He said he'd like to meet this friend of yours."

"Great!" Taylor replied. "When?"

"Six o'clock tomorrow morning at the Dimonthenes Café. He's to come alone and unarmed."

They paused again as the waitress returned and set a chilled tumbler of brandy in front of him. He paid her with a thousand-drachma piece and a smile. She smiled back at him, her blond hair shimmering with the glitter and chemicals she wore in it. The waitress cast a haughty look in Taylor's direction before sashaying away from the table.

"Alone I can guarantee, my sweet," Taylor replied, playing the role of a jilted lover, keeping her voice low enough that Midas had to lean forward to hear her. "But I don't know about unarmed. He's just recently out of prison, and there may be some people here in Athens who won't be so happy to see he's returned."

Midas gripped her hands in his and looked around before whispering, "Alone and unarmed. That's the deal." He inclined his head toward the door to reinforce his point. "They make those decisions, not me. I was not given a choice in the matter."

"I didn't say he wouldn't agree to it," Taylor said with a forced smile. "I just said that I can't guarantee he will."

"If he doesn't, then you need to let me know as soon as possible. My contact believes it's still risky to show his face so soon after an operation. He'd rather not if he has a choice."

"What operation?"

"Now, now," Midas said with a shake of his head. While he probably wasn't trying to sound like a condescending ass, he was doing a pretty good job of it. "You know I can't tell you that, my dearest Diona."

Taylor was using Diona Crysanthos for her cover name, posing as a broker of rare Greek art. Thus far, her story had seemed to satisfy Midas. Once she'd been informed about the impending arrival of the American, Taylor had wooed Midas into believing her half brother was returning to Greece and wanted to find some new action. Midas had been only too happy to oblige when he heard that Michalis was an expert with guns, explosives and most importantly paramilitary tactics. He'd spent the past eight years in an Argentine prison for theft and smuggling.

"Very well, I'll talk to him and let you know as soon as possible."

"When is he scheduled to arrive?"

"I'm not sure," she answered truthfully. "He was supposed to meet me at my place tonight. He said it was better that I not know what time exactly, just in case someone was waiting for him."

"Well, you know how to reach me." Midas downed the last of the drink he'd been nursing throughout their conversation.

Taylor tried to look surprised. "You're leaving?"

"Unfortunately," he said, sighing and shaking his head with anger. "The Parliament subcouncil convenes tonight, and my uncle has insisted I be there to cover it for the paper. He thinks it's time I start earning my way with Pontiki. I hope you're not too disappointed. I had planned to ask you to go with me on the Parthenon tour, since you hinted you've never seen it."

"That's okay, I'm very tired and I may be up late waiting on Michalis. Perhaps this weekend?"

"Yes," Midas replied with a mischievous smile. "That sounds like a wonderful compromise. Perhaps we may take a boat and tour the islands."

"It would be lovely," Taylor said throatily, although she was thinking how she wouldn't tour anything with the bloke on his best day.

He kissed her hand again before rising. "Until then, Flower."

Taylor finished her drink, waiting twenty minutes or so before leaving the club. Whatever Midas had up his sleeve, she was fairly convinced it had nothing to do with any political meeting. Politicians in Greece typically kept London Exchange hours, and it wouldn't have made any sense for them to convene at this hour unless there was some great emergency.

Then again, they might be meeting to discuss the kidnapping of Undersecretary Hyde-Baker. Her decision to travel to Thessaloníki before coming to Athens for the conference hadn't been the smartest one. She'd done it against numerous warnings, somehow convinced that if they kept it a secret she wouldn't be subject to danger. Information on British activity in this country spread far and wide. Nonetheless, she would have been much safer going straight to Athens.

As Taylor walked the few blocks to her apartment, she marveled at the architecture in this part of the city. The capital of Greece was a unique blend of historic and contemporary. It dominated the country in many facets, not the least of which included the economy, politics and culture. Athens was also home to much of Greece's industrial activity.

Taylor hadn't lied to Midas when she indicated her interest in seeing the Acropolis landmark. She'd spent several months in Greece but was left with very little time to tour the area. If her duties didn't have her probing for answers related to 17 November, then she was pulling administrative functions or other such silly busy work at the British embassy near Constitution Square. Never mind that just her very presence near the embassy could compromise her cover.

In any case, the man called Mike Belasko—aka Michalis Belapoulos—would be here soon and that would ease her mind some. She knew the Yanks had a lot of incompetents but word got around. This particular fellow was said to be very good, and Taylor believed it when she heard it from a direct source.

And former lover or not, if she couldn't bloody well trust the word of David McCarter, then whom could she trust?

AUDREY HYDE-BAKER squeezed her eyes shut and tried to imagine she was anywhere but where she was.

The odors wafting along the cool air were practically unbearable. Since she'd arrived bound and blindfolded, Hyde-Baker knew her chances of being found were lessening by the minute. There was really no practical way her people could free her if they couldn't even find her. And her captors obviously knew this, which explained why that particular terrorist—the dark-skinned one with the curly hair and beard—was so brazen with her at Thessaloníki.

She scolded herself for not listening to her security people.

Hyde-Baker couldn't help but wonder if these violent animals had already taken credit for their crimes. Had they kidnapped her for a ransom or was she just a political prisoner? The ambassador ultimately couldn't have cared less for her own life. But she was concerned that this group might have a hidden agenda; one that might have something to do with the upcoming conference. It dawned on her that she could be dealing with the very same group who had terrorized the land for so long.

Before she could speculate any further, the sound of footsteps echoed in her ears. Moments later, the blindfold was ripped from her face.

Hyde-Baker prepared herself to be blinded by the light, but as she opened her eyes she discovered it was still rather dark. The man with the beard now stood in front of her, studying her with a menacing grin. Behind those dark eyes was nothing but smug hate that lacked any warmth or character. The woman wondered if she weren't looking at a manifestation of evil itself.

A quick study of her surroundings revealed something of interest. As she suspected, they were deep underground. The network of sewer tunnels beneath Athens was dank and damp, which explained not only the lack of light but also the smell of human waste. Athens was a very dirty city with a poor economy. Most of the population was considered lower working class in her country. Air pollution was a serious problem aboveground. The Greek government had done little to either reclaim natural resources or accept outside help.

It didn't appear that things were much better in the subterranean world.

Hyde-Baker was bound to a metal chair. There were a few crates scattered along the tunnel with propane lanterns set on them. The little light they provided scattered ominous shadows across the walls, and Hyde-Baker did everything she could not to shudder. Her future looked bleak, at best.

"Well, Madam Secretary," the dark-haired stranger said, "I trust you're comfortable."

Hyde-Baker decided to remain silent.

"I will take that as a yes," he added.

She wasn't about to respond, but her curiosity got the better of her. "Who are you and what's the meaning of this?"

"The meaning of this will become very clear in a short time," the man retorted. He clasped his hands behind his back as he began to circle her chair. "My name is Cyril Helonas. I am a revolutionary for 17 November, and you are our prisoner."

"What do you want with me?" Hyde-Baker probed.

The man stopped hovering around her chair and smiled an even broader smile. "Oh, you will learn of that in good time. Right now, you are better advised to answer my questions and not offer resistance."

"What questions?"

The man reached out in a blinding moment and slapped her across the face. Hyde-Baker's head snapped sideways from the blow, and as the shock wore off the anger began to burn like the hot spot on her cheek. This Helonas was a brutal, evil man. One way or another he would eventually get his comeuppance. It was only a matter of time.

"I believe I just said it was you who would answer the questions," Helonas snapped, "not ask them. So unless a question is directed to you, keep your mouth shut!"

Hyde-Baker began to shake, and she bit her lip to quell the sensation. Fear rolled through her chest, stabbing her heart and sending her stomach on a roller-coaster ride. Nausea swept over her, and she could feel the bile rise in her throat with the lump. She resisted every impulse to vomit. She considered that perhaps she did value her life a little more than she thought.

"Now," Helonas continued calmly, "you have heard of the L3A, yes?"

"No," she replied in a cracked voice.

"Come now, Madam Secretary, we know you have," Helonas taunted her. "It is why you are here. Maybe I should refresh your memory. The L3A was approved by you, along with several other British and American diplomats, for design and manufacture by your government. As a matter of fact, I believe your stamp of approval was why Crown Arms of India began testing."

Hyde-Baker was astounded at the wealth of information this terrorist possessed. She and the NATO subcommittee had approved the design, manufacture and testing of the L3A. It was to be specifically licensed to groups such as Britain's SAS and MI-6, and for further bid to U.S. Navy SEALs, Special Forces and, most importantly, antiterrorist units in Greece. The deal was already signed and sealed for delivery of the first one thousand to Greek antiterrorist squads projected to be formed under the Sheringham Articles.

Very few members in any of the participating countries even knew of its existence, which meant Helonas was obviously well connected with higher-ups in the Greek government. That would confirm any question about sympathizers to 17 November within Parliament or the offices of the prime minister and his cabinet. The thought of government sympathizers within Greece—or any country that had suffered the kind of terrorist acts as this one—incensed her.

She had to find a way to stall them until she could plan an escape.

"I've heard rumors of the L3A," she lied. "But I have never been involved with approving or inventing weapons testing. Those matters are left to military advisers within the British parliament—"

"Don't lie to me," Helonas growled evenly. "We know you were part of the committee that approved this weapon, and we know what the intent was behind its invention."

"And what is that?" Hyde-Baker countered, immediately biting back a further response when she remembered the first blow he'd delivered.

It never came, but instead he replied, "You wish to subvert the aims of our organization and destroy the revolution. There are many who wish to do this, and for that I can overlook your transgressions. But we know that somewhere in Britain there is a factory manufacturing prototypes. I want to know where."

"I know of no such weapon," Hyde-Baker answered. "Or what you're even blathering about, Mr. Helonas."

Another blow was delivered to her, this time with Helonas's

fist. Hyde-Baker's head flew back and her tongue suddenly felt twice as thick. The sadistic bastard had nearly broken her jaw, and only the fact she could move it with a minimum of pain left her doubting he'd struck her hard enough to do any permanent damage.

"I do not believe that was what we wished to hear," Helonas warned. "I will ask you again. Where is the factory?"

"You can beat me to death if you wish!" Hyde-Baker barked, the pain of his brutality only strengthening her resolve. "But I cannot tell you what I do not know."

"Oh, I assure you that we will find out what you know, woman," Helonas said as he turned to leave. "And very soon, you will be happy to talk."

His laugh echoed in the labyrinthine corridors of the Athens underground as he disappeared down the tunnel.

Hyde-Baker let out a ragged breath, comfortable in the fact that Helonas had satisfied his lust for violence. At least she had procured some intelligent leads. The organization 17 November was definitely behind her kidnapping, and the measures being taken by NATO obviously had them concerned.

She also hoped someone would eventually come to rescue her. Perhaps members of MI-6 or the SAS. Her government wouldn't just leave her to die at the hands of these sadistic criminals. If they knew about her kidnapping and who was behind it, they would undoubtedly retaliate—and in force. Every concerted effort would be made by both British and American forces to facilitate her safe return. Maybe this was what had her captors on edge; they knew they were up against a superior force—a force to be reckoned with—and that panicked them. And they bloody damn well should be in a panic.

She could only pray that force, wherever it was, would find her in time.

The force known as Mack Bolan had arrived in Athens, and his mission wasn't starting as planned.

The night was cold and drizzly. While the summers in Greece were typically Mediterranean, the winters were usually wet. It was colder in the mountains, but this night there was a frosty bite to the December air that had settled on the valley plains of Athens.

Bolan watched Dina Taylor's house from an alleyway, melding with shadows as he observed the two men who'd followed her. Obviously, she hadn't seen them—either that or she was putting on a good show. For all he knew, she was behind the closed door with pistol in hand and waiting for them to make their move.

The Executioner reached to a shoulder holster beneath his black leather jacket and drew the Beretta 93-R and crossed the expanse, heading toward the short, wrought-iron fence that surrounded the house. He was able to travel under the cover of complete darkness since the streetlight appeared to be out.

Taylor had set up house in Neapolis, one of the better residential districts on the northeast side of Athens. The house was apparently financed by MI-6 to help maintain her cover as an art dealer. The British intelligence service had gone to great lengths to create that cover, piling layers of information into her file to keep prying eyes from discovering the real truth. It had been Barbara Price's professional opinion that even if 17 November had excellent contacts and sources of information, it would be difficult for them discover the truth about Taylor.

Apparently, somebody had because the two men trying to pick the door lock weren't there for tea and crumpets. Bolan effortlessly vaulted the fence at one corner and knelt. He watched for another minute, studying the deserted street and the houses. If the pair of watchers had backup, he didn't want to find out the hard way.

He didn't detect any movement.

Bolan waited until the men seemed focused on getting the door open before he crept toward them. It would be best to take them once they were inside, rather than start a commotion in the open. He didn't need the Greek police nipping at his heels and asking a lot of uncomfortable questions. The Executioner had never dropped the hammer on a cop—at least not a good cop—and he wasn't about to start.

The men whispered excitedly as the door swung inward and then moved into the darkness. Bolan waited until they were almost completely inside before he saw the flash of a muzzle through the doorway and heard a pop. One of the men fell onto the threshold and the other followed a millisecond later, jumping over his downed comrade to escape whatever had surprised them.

He saw Bolan on a fast approach and reached inside his trench coat. The Executioner tracked up with the muzzle of the Beretta and squeezed the trigger. The report of the 93-R wasn't much louder than the drops of water pelting Bolan's jacket. The 9 mm Parabellum round cored through the gunman's chest, ripping his aorta with considerable force. Bolan followed with a second shot to the head and moved past the body before it had collapsed.

The Executioner reached the porch and came through the doorway with pistol tracking, completely ignoring the dead man lying there. He came to face-to-face with Dina Taylor, and the two watched each other a moment before she lowered her weapon.

"Welcome to Greece, Mr. Belasko," she said with a smile.

THE ENGLISHWOMAN was beautiful, no question there.

But she was still inexperienced as hell, and the Executioner was wondering if this had been such a good idea after all. Bolan didn't mind playing by the rules when it was a matter of necessity, but this little alliance had been forced on him. He was a soldier doing a soldier's job—these kind of military operations were no place for an intelligence agent.

The fact Taylor was a woman had nothing to do with it, and Bolan would have argued that point with anyone who said otherwise. He'd known lots of capable women, allies who'd seen him through some real messes and even saved his neck on occasion. Many of them were ghosts now: Flor Trujillo, April Rose, Toby Ranger, Jütta Kaufmann. Some had survived the war and moved on; others had died; still others had just simply disappeared. But he couldn't forget any of them. They tugged on the strings of his heart and soul.

Bolan and Taylor had quickly wrapped the bodies in plastic tarps and brought them around to the back porch of the two-story house. Taylor indicated she would make arrangements to have them picked up by her people within the hour. The pair now sat at a kitchen table drinking very strong coffee. A map of the city was spread before them, and certain areas were marked in red pen.

"Any thoughts as to who those two might be working for?" Bolan said, peering at Taylor over the rim of his cup.

"Could be anyone," Taylor said, shaking her head as she stared absently at the map. "They might be some of Amphionides men, put on me through Midas."

"Who's Amphionides?"

"Deputy justice minister."

Bolan set down his coffee cup and shot her a hard look. "You mean the justice ministry of Greece? These men were secret police?"

"They might be police officers," she said angrily, "but there was nothing secret about them."

"I don't like killing cops, lady." Bolan shook his head and told her with frosty resolve, "I didn't find any police identification on them."

"And you wouldn't, if they're working for Amphionides personally."

"Tell me something," the Executioner said, somewhat confused now. "Why would a member of the Greek government cabinet want to assassinate you?"

"I don't know that they were here to assassinate me," she said. "They might have just come to ask questions."

Bolan waved at the front door. "By breaking into your house?"

"Look, Mr. Belasko, I don't know who they are or why they were here. Until my people can make a positive identification, I would think we have more important matters at hand."

"Maybe, but it would seem you shut them up before we could question them."

"I cannot risk anyone blowing my cover. Surely you can appreciate the position of my government. The retrieval of Undersecretary Hyde-Baker is tantamount to the success of the conference."

Bolan hated to admit it but Taylor was right. Brognola had also made it clear that cooperation with Taylor was part of the game plan, and he would need her to penetrate 17 November. To get her on the defensive wasn't wise.

"Tell me what you do know so far," the Executioner said.

"It's going to get damn bloody, Belasko," Taylor replied. "I can feel it. This whole meet smells like a setup."

"Well, it's been your show with this Midas guy for the last month or two. What's your take on him?"

"Midas?" she said, snorting. "He's a follower. Hell, he's the bloody follower of a follower."

"He's connected well enough to know people inside 17 November," Bolan reminded her.

Taylor's smug expression changed to one of new realization.

The soldier knew he'd struck a chord and made it clear to Taylor that she wasn't dealing with any Johnny-come-lately. Then again, she'd probably known that if Bolan's information from McCarter was any indication. Taylor's experience with the SAS gave her quite a background in paramilitary tactics, but it didn't make her an expert. Nonetheless, Bolan saw a promising career for Taylor if she didn't let arrogance or carelessness get in the way.

"Okay, I'll give you that point," Taylor conceded. "But he's no master criminal."

"What's his connection with these revolutionaries?"

"He's a journalist for Pontiki, a local newspaper that primarily deals with government news and how that relates to the rest of the world."

"A political paper?"

Taylor shrugged. "More or less, I suppose. I have one here if you'd like to see it."

"Sorry," Bolan said with a smile. "I forgot my Greek dictionary."

"Not that it would probably help you anyway," Taylor shot back. She smiled a good-natured smile and added, "Most of the population here are ethnic, and they speak Demotike, the modern Greek vernacular."

"I understand French and English are spoken widely, too."

"Yes," she said with a nod. "I don't think you'll need me along on your meeting to translate."

"What have you told Midas about me?"

Taylor rose to get the carafe on the counter and poured each of them more coffee before she answered him. "Only that you're my half brother and just out of prison. He knows you deal in stolen art, that you've fenced a piece or two for me over the years, and he thinks you're part Greek."

"This is going to be tough," the Executioner admitted. "Seeing as I'm supposed to be posing as a Greek native but can't speak the language."

"Easily explained," Taylor replied. "You were born here and moved to England with our mother before age six. She married and that's when they had me. You have no idea who or where your father is. You don't have an accent because you left London at twelve to travel with our mother, who was also an art dealer. I stayed home with father. When she died, you were eighteen and you took care of yourself. You joined the British Expeditionary Forces but were eventually booted out for insubordination and stealing explosives."

"And then I ended up in prison in Argentina for art theft?"

"Yes. You spent eight years there, but you have a reputation for being an expert with demolitions and paramilitary tactics." She arched an eyebrow and gave him an appraising look for the first time. "A role I don't happen to think you'll have much trouble settling into."

Bolan shrugged. "Role camouflage is easy if you know your enemy."

"Agreed, except in this case we don't know the enemy all that well. Despite his connections, Midas is a romantic. He fancies himself a real Romeo. Hardly what I would deem terrorist material. But the members of 17 November have evaded capture for almost thirty years."

"Yeah," Bolan replied, "but I know the type because I've spent many years fighting them. I should be able to pull it off." He looked down at the map. "Where's the meet scheduled?"

Taylor leaned forward, and Bolan was suddenly aware of her closeness. She was wearing a pretty low-cut blouse, and the curves of her breasts were plainly visible. She wore some kind of sweet-smelling perfume, although not too much, and even up that close there didn't seem to be a single imperfection in her cream-colored skin. The nearness of her was almost heady, and Bolan forced himself to keep things in serious perspective.

"The place is known," she began, pointing to a spot on the map, "as Dimonthenes Café. Here."

"Near the outskirts of the city," Bolan observed.

"A bit, I suppose, but not totally. It's actually near the road that leads up to the Acropolis. As you can see, the area here is called Plaka."

"Which is?"

Taylor leaned back in her seat and showed an expression of uncertainty that did nothing to impose on her graceful features. "It's the old neighborhood of Athens. Quite actually, it encircles the Acropolis. Very picturesque and old-world looking, I'd say. Houses are small and single story, with villas and narrow streets and the like. I've always thought it was beautiful. But it's bloody crowded."

Bolan frowned. "Doesn't sound like the kind of place for a private meet."

"You're supposed to be there early, 0600 hours, Midas said. The places won't be crowded yet. Things don't really start hopping down there until about 0900. Plenty of time for you to meet and conclude your business."

"What's the plan?"

"Someone in their ranks is going to meet you and size you up. Word from Midas has it they need a military tactician, and they're willing to interview any possible takers."

"So I just happened to volunteer, huh?"

"In a way. You're supposed to be a real hotshot. Full of the damn Greek machismo, lady killer sort of bunkum. You must remember that you're dealing with people of very similar beliefs to those I just described. Some of the members within 17 November are said to be women. They are a small, close-knit group, according to what Midas has told me, and they are freely radical. While they call themselves revolutionaries, they are really quite counterrevolutionary in their goals. They're iconoclasts of conventional Greek society and particularly violent against outside interference that results in variations of the same."

"Greek puritans to the last," Bolan remarked.

"Terrorists, to the last, Yank."

"Touché. What about terms?"

"Alone and unarmed."

"No dice," said the Executioner, shaking his head. "I'm not going in there unarmed."

"I told my contact you'd say that."

"You told him right."

Taylor leaned forward again and rested a delicate hand on Bolan's knee. "Look, you can't cross these people or the deal's off. If you're going to make this happen, it's going to have to be on their terms. At least coming out of the gate. You have to be willing to show good faith."

"Maybe I'll go armed anyway. They'd be expecting that, and they'll pat me down, take the gun, et cetera."

"I don't care if you go with a gun or not," Taylor replied. She rose and disappeared in a back room, returning a moment later with a long case. She set it on the table, flipped open three latches and lifted the lid.

Inside was a true work of art. It was an Accuracy International L-96 A-1, the official sniping rifle of the British army. One of its most prominent features was the aluminum-and-outer-plastic frame configured to support the action and the free-floating barrel. This particular design made it a highly balanced and efficient weapon. It had four-groove rifling in a 654 mm barrel, and was configured in several variations.

Bolan whistled and looked up at Taylor with surprise. He jerked his head at the rifle and asked, "You know how to use it?"

"I've qualified as an expert every time on the thousand-meter course at SAS proving grounds. I was an Olympic contender for Britain under an assumed name, of course."

"I'm sure."

"I was also a brunette then," she added, pulling her long, golden strands behind her ear.

"Go figure," Bolan quipped. He changed to a more conversational tact and said, "Tell me how you know David."

Something in her look changed dramatically, and Bolan wasn't sure if it was for better or worse. He'd obviously touched a nerve while trying to find some common ground. McCarter hadn't mentioned anything about their relationship one way or another, but the Executioner saw something in Taylor's face that signaled more than friendship had been involved.

"Sorry," he hastened to add. "I didn't know it was a sore subject."

"It's not, Yank," she said. "It's just a closed one."

"Fair enough." Bolan nodded at the rifle and added, "And just what do you plan to do with this?"

"I know exactly where Dimonthenes Café is," she replied triumphantly, cocking her head and looking at Bolan with surprise. "I also know where there's some excellent rooftop cover about a hundred meters away, give or take. This particular model is known as the Covert PM, which means it has an integral suppressor. If there's any trouble, I'll be ready for it. All you have to do is duck."

"It would appear I misjudged you, lady," Bolan admitted.

"That's quite all right, Belasko," she said with a cocksure grin. "It happens all the bloody time."

The meet was set and Bolan was ready.

He could practically feel Taylor watching him through the crosshairs of the rifle scope as he sat at an open-air table. Taylor's description of Plaka had done it justice; the place definitely had the old-world look.

The Dimonthenes Café was set in a crusty building that looked as if it might collapse at any moment. The street and sidewalks were devoid of activity. It was so quiet that the chirps of birds that alighted on lamps and rooftops were deafening. Even the table at which he sat was made from cheap sheet metal that wouldn't have stopped an air-gun pellet, let alone a bullet.

Given the sparse surroundings, the soldier realized he'd have nowhere to go for cover if things went awry. He'd have to rely on Taylor's skill with that rifle. He hadn't put that kind of trust in someone for a long time. Usually, it was the Executioner behind the trigger—now the roles were reversed.

Bolan didn't like this one bit. The weight of the Beretta beneath his jacket was his only solace. The echo of Brognola's words came back to him, and he couldn't shake the feeling he was entering a trap.

He squinted into the sun as a solitary figure stepped from the cover of a building at an intersection down the street. The

Executioner could see it was a man, but he couldn't tell if the guy was armed. He glanced at his watch—the new arrival was about ten minutes late, and Bolan tried to shake his aggravation.

The man's gait was relaxed but purposeful as he drew near. Bolan laid aside his apprehension and concentrated, every sense alert to danger. He let his eyes dance across the buildings, watching the shadows for any sudden movement, all the time keeping his sense of distance to the man.

The sound of scraping feet behind him caused Bolan to stand and turn as he reached for the Beretta. He spun in time to see the barrel of a machine pistol leveled at his chest from a distance of five yards.

"Hold it right there," the gunner snapped.

The woman was lithe with long, dark hair and brown eyes. She was dressed in black jeans and a faded green halter top beneath a leather overcoat. It was warm for that time of morning, and Bolan figured she'd worn the coat to conceal the AKSU-74 she had trained on him.

The woman looked to her right and whispered, "Adonis, search him."

A small, muscular man in slacks and a white, ill-fitted shirt stepped from the shadows of an adjoining building and frisked Bolan. He pushed the soldier's hand away and relieved him of the Beretta, completed his search and then looked at the woman and nodded.

"Have a seat," she said.

The female gunner hit the ground, her chest suddenly exploding from the impact of a 7.62 mm round.

The Executioner mentally began to curse Taylor, turning back toward the man, who had stopped about twenty yards from the table. The look on his face registered his sense that they had been betrayed.

The guy holding Bolan's Beretta was the next to fall under Taylor's marksmanship. The man's head snapped sideways as the force of the round ripped out his jaw. The Beretta flew from his fingers and clattered to the pavement as a second round punched through his chest. The Beretta was followed a moment later by the body of the man called Adonis.

A whistle echoed through the air.

Bolan reached down and retrieved his Beretta before he saw a half-dozen police officers charge down the street toward him, coming from the same direction as the stranger had come. The man turned and saw them, as well, then began to run toward Bolan.

The Executioner took only a split second to make a decision. "It's a trap!" he told the man rushing him.

The man blew past Bolan, his hair flopping in the breeze. "Follow me!"

The soldier followed him around the corner of the café and into an alleyway where the man and woman had first made their appearance. They sprinted along the narrow strip until they reached a set of metal steps that descended to a door. The man led Bolan through that door into the darkness. The air was cooler here, and the Executioner could hear the sound of running water.

As they walked toward a wall, Bolan listened for their pursuers. There were no sounds other than those of their own footsteps. The man reached a point in the wall and instructed Bolan to help him as he pushed on it. The Executioner complied, not wanting to risk asking questions. There would be time for that later. The wall gave suddenly under their weight and moved inward. The man slipped inside and Bolan followed him.

Behind the wall was a metal frame attached to a hydraulic arm. The tube glistened with a coat of fresh grease. Together, they pushed the makeshift wall into place. The man gestured for Bolan to follow and the soldier got into step behind him. The pair traversed a dark corridor covered by a damp sheen—droplets ran down portions of the walls, and there was the faintest sound of running water somewhere ahead.

The two continued at a quickened pace. They walked about five hundred yards before the man stopped and turned to Bolan. He clutched a Walther P-38 and pointed it in Bolan's face. The big American forced himself to look calm and raised his hands in surprise.

"Let's not jump to conclusions here, pal," he told the man coolly.

The gunman had curly black hair and eyes that were like twin pools of hot tar. He was ruggedly handsome, not in a suave manner but rather a macho sense. The man studied Bolan for several moments, but the pistol didn't waver.

The soldier knew he'd never reach his Beretta in time, and he continued to stand there and watch the man.

"If I thought you had something to do with these events," the gunman said, "you would be dead already."

"I don't know what happened back there, but you saved my neck." Bolan held out his hand. "I owe you."

The man studied him a moment longer and then slowly holstered his weapon. He shook Bolan's hand and replied, "My name is Cyril Helonas."

"Michalis Belapoulos." Bolan replied in a friendly tone.

Helonas had a firm grip and he tried to impress the Executioner with it, but Bolan wasn't going to play that game. He gripped Helonas's hand just as firmly, and he could tell his new ally was trying ignore the discomfort. With the formalities dispensed, Helonas folded his arms and began walking.

"We took a great risk to meet you like this, Michalis," Helonas said. "And yet you came armed anyway."

"I'm sure the risk was shared," Bolan countered. "You didn't follow the rules yourself. At least I came alone."

"Quite right," Helonas said. Now he grinned and nodded to show his concession. "I have learned to be careful in my business. Just as I'm sure you have."

"Caution always worked for me," Bolan replied, "until recently."

"Do you think someone set us up?"

"I wouldn't doubt it. Maybe it was this Midas guy."

Helonas snorted. "I don't think so."

"How can you be sure?"

"He is my cousin. I have trusted him with such matters before, and he's always come through. I do not think he betrayed us."

"I made some enemies here in my time," Bolan offered. "Maybe the police were after me."

"Yes, that is a matter which puzzles us." Helonas made a quizzical expression.

Bolan noted his use of the plural form and referenced it. Intelligence reports were accurate—17 November really did operate in a team concept.

"As I understand it, you spent the past few years in Argentina. Incarcerated there, were you not?"

"Yeah." Bolan attempted to look like they were in uncomfortable territory as part of the act.

"I had a friend down there," Helonas continued. "Perhaps you knew him?"

Bolan could sense this guy baiting him. It was pretty unlikely he would have known anybody in an Argentine prison, but this was a fact he couldn't have foreseen. He'd have to play the next few moments by ear. "What was his name?"

"Daemon Papandreou."

Bolan shook his head. "Never heard of him."

"Really," Helonas said. "Maybe that is because he died ten years ago."

"I was only there for eight years."

"Ah, I see. My contacts said you were arrested for smuggling stolen goods out of the country. Artwork, as I understand it." Helonas shrugged and stopped to face him. "But we must play these little games. You understand, yes?"

"No, but who cares," Bolan snapped, already tiring of the small talk. "Look, pal, my specialty is military tactics. You happen to be looking for someone with that expertise and I happen to be unemployed. Do you want me or do I walk?"

Something dark and dangerous changed in Helonas's face, but the Executioner wouldn't let it affect him. Helonas was probably a genius, and that made him very dangerous. But if Bolan planned to get inside 17 November, he would have to act the part and show the man he wasn't afraid of anyone or anything.

"I see you like to be direct," Helonas said.

"Why mince words?"

"You don't have an accent. You were raised in London?"

"Until I was ten. Most of the time I traveled with my mother."

Helonas turned and started walking again. "Diona Crysanthos is your sister?"

"Half sister," Bolan replied. "Same mother but different fathers."

Helonas smiled and inspected his fingernails. "I see your mother got around."

Now it was Bolan's turn to look dangerous. "Is it customary for you to go around insulting a guy's mother, or are you just looking for a fight?"

The Executioner's reply sank in because Helonas stopped again and leaned close. He gestured for Bolan to do the same and put his hands behind his back to show there was no threat. The soldier leaned in close enough to feel the heat from Helonas's breath.

"Good. I sense you're a patriotic man, one who understands family and loyalty. This would indicate you're an idealist with vision. I think you're exactly who we're looking for."

Bolan smiled with frosty indignation. "Does that mean I pass?"

"Not completely. There is one more small test that everyone must undergo. If you think you're up to the challenge, we may proceed to the next phase. If not, I go my way and you may go yours."

"I owe you my life," Bolan said, stroking Helonas's ego. "A life-debt is something I take very serious, Cyril."

Helonas smiled and nodded. "Then follow me."

DINA TAYLOR WATCHED the road in her rearview mirror as she drove back to Neapolis. She was angry with herself for being so sloppy and unprofessional. Once she'd dropped the woman, she had to put down the man, as well. The British agents who'd picked up the bodies the night before had warned her to be wary of Midas.

She wished now that she'd listened to them.

There was no question in her mind who was behind this ambush. Midas was the only one who could have blown the whistle. His connections with Deputy Justice Minister Amphionides pointed the finger of blame. He had ample opportunity to contact his uncle, and it would explain why he was adamant about Taylor contacting him if Belasko had turned down the meet.

There was no one else who stood to gain something by blowing this deal. Belasko and his contact weren't even suspect; the American's people didn't ring true and nobody in MI-6 actually knew about the details of the meet; finally, it was unlikely there was a mole planted inside 17 November who could have set them up. That left only Midas as the guilty party.

Taylor arrived at her place and parked in the attached garage. She emptied the contents of the trunk, including the rifle and the spent shells. She'd only fired three shots and didn't want to leave any evidence that the Greek police could trace back to her government. British operatives in the country were already unappreciated, as were their operations. It wouldn't do for her to start a bloody scandal and make a large problem larger.

Once she'd cleaned the rifle and put it away, Taylor left the house and walked a few blocks to a bus stop. She used the pay phone there to arrange a meet with her supervisor, leaving him an encrypted message with the secretary, and then boarded a bus for Constitution Square.

Taylor sat in the rearmost seat, watching the face of every person who got on or off. She couldn't trust anyone now, and she had to proceed cautiously without becoming paranoid. The little meet between Belasko and Midas's contact hadn't gone off as planned. That left a lot of unanswered questions, and Taylor needed advice from someone that she trusted.

That someone was Sir Radley Holcomb Brygmart, her case officer and mentor. Sir Brygmart had taken a rather fatherly role when it came to Taylor. He was her confidant and adviser in all intelligence matters, as much as he was her superior officer. Actually, it was Brygmart who had originally recommended Taylor for duty in Her Majesty's secret service. He'd first seen Taylor's capabilities in a joint operation of MI-6 and SAS personnel during the Gulf War. She'd been quite a little pistol at that time, full of patriotic fervor and idealism.

But her talents would be of better service—or so Sir Brygmart told the deputy prime minister—in MI-6. Taylor was honored when she was requested to report for duty to MI-6 headquarters by "orders of the highest level." If Her Majesty needed Taylor for duty within MI-6, then so be it. After six years of honorable service, Taylor had never regretted her decision to accept what she viewed as a promotion.

And neither had Brygmart regretted it, a point so obvious when he sat down next to her on the park bench and smiled graciously. He was tall and lean, with cropped white hair and puffy cheeks. He had the kind of warm and generous face that made people comfortable, something that Taylor had felt since the moment she'd laid eyes on him.

He planted a kiss on her cheek—like a father and daughter might greet one another—then it was down to business. "How are you, my dear?"

"Not good, sir," Taylor replied honestly. "There was some trouble early this morning in Plaka."

"I heard something of this," Brygmart replied, raising an eyebrow. "I surmise from your tone that you were involved?"

She looked down at her hands and nodded. "Yes, sir. I was operating under orders to work with the Americans in the kidnapping of Undersecretary Hyde-Baker. I think my contact blew us."

Brygmart sighed and looked into the distance, not really appearing to focus on anything in particular. "What makes you think that?"

"Deductive reasoning," Taylor replied with certainty. She looked at him and added, "I'm convinced he was the only one who stood to gain from this. His connections with Amphionides make him a strong candidate, as well."

"But you don't have any proof," Brygmart concluded, summing up the problem in a statement.

"No, sir," Taylor murmured.

"Then we cannot allow our prejudices to overtake our common sense, my dear. There is no question that your contact is the most likely candidate. But that doesn't give us carte blanche to accuse the deputy justice minister of conspiring with terrorists and criminals."

"I understand, sir."

"What was your contact's name?"

"I only know him as Midas," Taylor said, ashamed to admit she didn't know more than that. "He would never tell me his last name. I do know that he's Amphionides's nephew and that he works as a journalist for Pontiki."

"Very well," Brygmart retorted. "I will personally look into this matter. Wait to hear from me. In the meantime, I would suggest you keep your head down."

Taylor nodded.

"Did you leave anything at this meeting that the authorities here could trace back to us?"

"No, Sir Brygmart," Taylor said, shaking her head. "I made sure the place was clean before I left."

"Good." On afterthought he said, "We identified your two visitors from last night. They're common thugs, wanted by Greek police for a score of crimes."

"Do you have any idea who they were working for or what they wanted?" Taylor asked.

"We're not sure, but we'll continue to work on it until a solution presents itself. What became of the agent we asked the Americans to send?"

"I don't know, sir. He disappeared with his contact during the incident in Plaka and I did not see him after that. I cannot assume he's dead."

"Yes, you can," Brygmart warned her with a hoarse whisper. He stared at her now with soft but determined blue eyes. "You must not make any attempt to contact him. If the meet was blown, then members with 17 November will assume this man is a liability and kill him. It will do no good for you to interfere."

"But what if he is alive, sir?"

Brygmart shook his head emphatically. "It doesn't matter if he's alive or not. More than likely, he's dead. But even if he manages to conjure a cover story, they're going to be watching him closely. Any attempts he makes to reach you, or vice versa, could prove disastrous. They would kill him and most likely the undersecretary, as well. You must stay away for her sake."

"And what if he does try to make contact?"

"Then you are to break it off and find me." Brygmart smiled. "We cannot risk the life of Undersecretary Hyde-Baker for the welfare of one American agent, no matter what you might feel about that."

"But, sir," Taylor protested, "this man was sent to help us. We've been entrusted with his well-being. It would be wrong to just leave him hanging if he needs our help. It would be...it would be traitorous!"

Brygmart raised his hand and looked around. Taylor realized she was talking too loud and also took in their surroundings with a watchful eye. It didn't appear anyone was the least bit interested in their conversation. Then again, 17 November had spies everywhere, as did the Greek government—nothing was kept secret for long in Athens.

"I apologize, sir," Taylor said. "I forget my place."

He grinned and placed a hand on her arm that she knew was meant to be a sign of forgiveness and comfort. "It's all right, Dina. This is why I recommended you for the secret service. You are, without question, one of the most outspoken women I have ever met. I liked that about you from the first moment I met you in Kuwait."

Taylor smiled and felt herself blush. "I know you're only looking out for me, sir. You've been like a father to me and you've never rendered a bit of bad advice. But I'm not sure I can turn my back on the Yank. It would be heartless and unprofessional."

"If you disobey me, Dina," Brygmart said, "you could destroy everything we've worked for here in the past few months. Promise me that you'll do as I ask. If you go outside my wishes, I will not be able to protect you."

"I promise, sir," Taylor whispered. "I promise."

But Taylor didn't believe herself even as she heard the words come out of her mouth.

Mack Bolan stood inside the circle and studied the people surrounding him.

There were about twenty of them—twenty-five tops by a quick count. They stared at him, men and women alike, tall and short, dark haired and blond, thin and fat. It was a motley assemblage, but they had one thing in common: they worked with a unity and cohesion that had transformed 17 November into one of the most elusive and dangerous terrorist organizations in the world.

"Michalis Belapoulos," Cyril Helonas's voice echoed from somewhere within the huge room beneath the city streets, "you are standing in a kyklos ek chronos."

"A circle of time," Bolan muttered, surprised when Helonas stepped from the crowd.

"You know your Greek," Helonas answered him. "A bit surprising since you haven't been to your home since you were but an infant."

Bolan showed him a frosty smile. "I had lots of time to practice in Argentina."

Helonas nodded and then began to walk around the edge of the circle.

The soldier noticed that everyone was careful to stay outside of it. Not one set of toes crossed the line. The circle was carved into the smooth stone of the floor. Inside of it was the triangle, or Delta sign, and above the face of each side of the triangle was a letter from the alphabet. The circle had an area of maybe 115 feet, give or take.

Another man stepped from the crowd—this one stood half again as tall as Helonas with muscles that rippled along his arms and chest. He was one of the biggest men the Executioner had ever seen, but oddly he had a gentle face. The guy's hands could have ripped most normal men in two, and Bolan was quickly beginning to surmise just what this little test Helonas had referred to would consist of.

"What's with Brutus here?" Bolan inquired, looking up at the behemoth.

Helonas chuckled and put his hand on the big man's arm. "This is Endre. He is one of our oldest members and our most faithful messenger. Endre will be looking after you for the next few days, to make sure you do not betray us. It would not do for us to have a traitor in our midst."

The Executioner looked at Endre and nodded.

Endre didn't speak or even flinch. He just folded his arms and growled under his breath.

"Thanks, Helonas," Bolan said, "but I don't need a baby-sitter."

"You do if you wish to be called one of us, Michalis," Helonas warned. "Endre is here only to make sure you obey. This is the other test I spoke of...a test of loyalty." He looked at the group and smiled. "However, there is an alternative."

Bolan became simultaneously suspicious and curious. "And what's that?"

"You may challenge Endre to a test of strength and skill, here and now. If you can defeat him, you are free to come and go just as the rest of us."

"I fight only when necessary," Bolan shot back. "This isn't a game to me."

"Nor to us, Michalis. Once you have done the first job and

perhaps the second, then, and only then, will we feel we can trust you."

"Fine," Bolan agreed.

The soldier didn't like it but he knew there was little he could do about it. Endre was here to stay, and Bolan had nothing to say about it. Even if he could have overpowered the big lug—and he knew he probably could, given the fact that the weakness in men that size was their speed—he had no desire to raise alarms in Helonas. Or in the rest of the group, for that matter. He would need their trust if he were to successfully destroy them from the inside.

Bolan was going to have to pose as a team player, and he could only hope that whatever they asked him to do wasn't going to complicate matters or cost innocent lives. Then again, neither his nor Audrey Hyde-Baker's luck would hold out forever, so if he was going to make a move against 17 November it would have to be soon.

"What's the first job?" Bolan pressed.

"Come with us," Helonas said, gesturing toward Endre.

He dispersed the rest of the crowd and they sauntered away. Some of the men in the group looked disappointed, and Bolan wondered if they hadn't been hoping for the Executioner to accept Helonas's challenge, as well as a beating from Endre. Well, Endre would just have to wait for another opportunity to tear some other unfortunate soul limb from limb, because Bolan wasn't about to let him.

The threesome left the area and walked down another tunnel to a well-lighted work area. Some large wooden crates lying about served as desks along with milk crates and buckets as seats. A score of propane lanterns—some hanging from spikes in the walls and others resting on crates—kept the place bright and cast ominous shadows throughout the length of the tunnel.

Helonas led Bolan to one of the makeshift desks and pulled some information from a cardboard tube. He unrolled a map of a city and the blueprints of a building, neither of which the Executioner recognized. Bolan leaned over the crate and studied the plans a minute before looking at Helonas for an explanation.

"It's a foundation and structure plan for a diplomatic building that houses staff to the prime minister's cabinet."

Bolan nodded. "And the town?"

"The building is located in Pátrai. You are familiar with this area, no?"

Bolan nodded. "Somewhat. Like you said, I haven't been here since I was a kid. But I know that Pátrai is located in the northeast, a port city on the Gulf of Corinth if I'm not mistaken."

"Very good," Helonas replied, slapping Bolan on the back. He looked at Endre and added, "He knows his geography if he doesn't know anything else, eh?"

Endre nodded and for the first time he smiled. But the grin faded when Bolan looked at him. The Executioner shrugged the matter away. It seemed Endre was to keep up appearances until the rest of the group decided they trusted Bolan.

"What's my part in this?"

"You're the tactician," Helonas retorted matter-of-factly. "You will formulate a plan to get us inside so we can plant charges, and then you're going to rig the thing to blow." Helonas raised his hands, shrugged and added, "Simple! Eh?"

"Not necessarily," Bolan said, shaking his head.

Helonas looked puzzled. He stared hard at the Executioner and asked, "What do you mean?"

"I mean, you're going to need some pretty heavy stuff to knock out supports of this size," Bolan replied, pointing at the map.

"We have several hundred pounds of C-4 plastique," Helonas replied.

"It won't be enough," Bolan announced, sitting back on the bucket and folding his arms.

"What do you mean it will not be enough?"

"Look, I may not know a lot about your operations yet," Bolan stated, "but I do know one thing and that's explosives. Did you see how thick those columns are?" The Executioner shook his head with conviction. "It's going to take quite a bit to level that thing. A lot more than just some C-4."

"How much more?"

"Depends on what you use," the Executioner replied, shrugging. "A quarter ton of ammonium nitrate in the right places would probably do the job nicely. But being this is a political building attached to the Greek cabinet, security will be heavy. Even if I could level that place, we'd still have to get all of that equipment by them. Not easy at all, Cyril."

"Well, you are our new tactician. We're paying you to help us," he replied. "What do you suggest?"

"Who are you paying?" Bolan replied, pinning Helonas with an ice-blue stare. "I haven't seen a dime yet."

Helonas looked at Endre, then Bolan, and back and forth that way for a few moments. Finally, he reached into his pants pocket and withdrew a wad of Greek money. He counted out the equivalent of ten thousand U.S. dollars and threw it into Bolan's lap.

"We have some explosives here, which will be a start," Helonas said. "You can use that to buy anything else you might need. You may keep any left over as compensation or use it for bribes. I do not care how you spend it, my friend. Just do what you must to make this happen."

Helonas turned to leave them alone.

"When are you planning to do the job?" Bolan asked.

"Tomorrow night," Helonas murmured.

The Executioner nodded, and he registered something between agitation and disgust on Helonas's face. He called after the terrorist and the man stopped and whirled. He looked at the soldier but there was a hard edge to his expression.

Bolan held up the wad of cash and shook his head. "It's not about this, Cyril. It's about the job. I do this for the sake of our people, you know? Don't forget that."

A disarming grin broke through Helonas's anger and he began to laugh. As he turned to continue on his way, he slapped his thigh and said, "I see a long and happy future for you in our group, Michalis."

The Executioner couldn't say he felt the same way.

"I DO NOT LIKE this," Endre said as they parked the car in front of Dina Taylor's house.

It was the first time the man had spoken to the Executioner.

"What would you like?" Bolan argued. "Look, I can't get this job done if I don't have the right stuff. Cyril said to buy what we need. This person has the contacts to do that, so quit worrying about it and let's go."

Bolan exited the car before Endre could offer any other protests; the Greek giant had no choice but to follow him. Somehow, Bolan was going to have to get a message to Taylor and he'd found a spare moment—when Endre wasn't looking over his shoulder—to get that message to her. He'd written down the basic plan on one piece of paper over another, pressing hard so that everything he wrote would be legible when dusted or brushed with pencil lead. Then, he listed the stuff he would need on that second sheet, using a very bright light to view the practically invisible marks as he wrote between them.

Then he gave the paper to Endre.

"What's this for?" the giant asked him.

"That's the list of equipment I'll require. You can see what's on it and give it to my contact yourself. This way, you're my witness to the group that I didn't pass anything else."

Endre nodded with satisfaction and Bolan knew the bait was set. Reaching Taylor and getting her the information wasn't the problem now. The only problem would be whether she could acquire the stuff he needed in time, and how she would get the message that there was something hidden between those lines.

They walked up the sidewalk and through the front gate. Bolan led Endre around to the back, insisting that they not make contact with Taylor where others might see them. The Executioner was counting on the fact that Endre didn't know Taylor, and the fact she had contacts with the underworld wouldn't make a bit of difference. Ultimately, however, Bolan knew it probably didn't matter. How he got his material probably didn't make a damn bit of difference to 17 November as long as they could accomplish their goals.

Still, it stretched the limits of his credibility when Bolan—posing as a supposed expert—would have to use his alleged half sister as a source for equipment. That was okay, though, because he already had an answer prepared if Helonas or anyone else decided to question him.

The soldier rapped on the door and Taylor answered it a few seconds later. She covered her shock pretty well, turning it into surprise as she reached out and hugged him.

"Michalis!" she said. "How long has it been?"

"Too long," the Executioner told her. He turned and nodded to Endre. The man stepped forward and handed the list to her. "I need the stuff on that list. You think you can reach out to your associates and get it for me?"

Taylor took the list hesitantly, dropping her smile and watching Endre with a cautious expression. She opened the paper and studied it, then whistled softly and looked at Bolan.

"That's a pretty tall order, Michalis," she said. "When do you need it?"

"Tonight."

"Ah," she replied, nodding and looking at the list again. "Rush job, eh?"

"Come on, we have an agreement," Bolan said gruffly, seeing his opening and nodding at the list. "No questions and no reading between the lines. Got it?"

"Yeah," she said, her face going flat like a cool professional as she folded the paper and stuffed it into the pocket of her jeans. "I got it. When and where?"

"That depends," Bolan said. "First, I need to know if you can do it."

"I'm pretty sure."

"Pretty sure doesn't cut it. Can you or can't you?"

"Okay, okay, I'll get your stuff," she said. "Do you have the money with you?"

Bolan nodded, reached into his pocket, withdrew the money Helonas had given him and pressed it into Taylor's hand. "Will that cover it?"

She counted it quickly and then nodded as she stuffed it into the same pocket where she'd put the list. Bolan could only pray that Taylor was smart enough to pick up on his signal, and she'd look for the hidden message. "It should. You still haven't said when and where."

Bolan shrugged and looked at Endre. "You know this town better than I do. Any ideas?"

"Do you know where the Benaki Museum is?" Endre asked.

"Of course," Taylor shot back.

"Be there at 8:00 o'clock sharp tonight," he instructed her. "Leave a car containing the merchandise at the gate with the attendant. He will give you a ticket for the vehicle. Go inside the museum, wait one half hour. When you come out you may retrieve your car. We will have it unloaded and be gone by then."

"I understand."

Bolan breathed a sigh of relief as she closed the door and they walked back to Endre's car. The first phase of his plan was under way.

THE MEETING WENT OFF without a hitch, although the Executioner hadn't been allowed to participate. He'd argued this point with Helonas and other members of the group—he was the only one who could insure they got the right stuff after all. But several members said they couldn't be completely impartial when it came to trusting him, and expressed concerns he was allowed too much freedom too soon.

Helonas heeded their words and forced Bolan to stay behind while the others did the exchange.

The Executioner could only hope that Taylor had gotten the message.

He thought of her now as he sat with Endre, Helonas and two others aboard a train car bound for the port city of Pátrai. The main rail line came south out of Bulgaria and went to Athens by way of Thessaloníki. From there, it proceeded west through Elevsís and Megara until it reached Kórinthos. It then turned toward the northwest, and the only other stop would be Aiyion before it reached Pátrai.

Train travel was very common in Greece because of accessibility and affordability. Commuting by train was as economical and commonplace as it was across many parts of Europe. Then again, most of the countryside was rural, and sometimes traveling to the more remote areas by train was the option for people who considered automobiles a luxury only for the very influential or rich.

In many respects it was a very simple way of life—an uncomplicated existence that most Americans probably took for granted. The thought of not owning a car or the inability to travel freely due to financial constraints would have appalled most Americans. Those who had never done without couldn't appreciate it when such simple amenities were taken from them and not because of legal considerations, but merely because they didn't have enough money.

It was a sad existence, and the Executioner understood why the actions of groups like 17 November only made it worse. Not only could no one travel because they couldn't afford it, but now they didn't want to travel out of fear they might get blown up or gunned down in the process. The people he sat among had caused untold misery in the lives of innocents, and Bolan would insure that every one of them paid for it.

The thought only strengthened his resolve to end the seeds of horror sown by these terrorists.

And then there was locating Hyde-Baker and getting her out alive.

He hadn't seen her, although the soldier was certain they had her. They'd taken credit for it, and no other group had come forward to renounce that claim. There was little reason for them to lie about it anyway, and Bolan could picture Helonas as the type of man who would torment the woman. He could see him taunting her, teasing her with the thought of her release if she told him whatever it was he wanted to know.

What Bolan couldn't understand, and nobody had been able to deduce was the reason behind Hyde-Baker's kidnapping. Other than a bargaining tool, she had no value to them—unless she knew something that Bolan didn't. At some point the

Executioner knew he would have to locate her and help her escape. It was more than likely that's when he'd blow his own cover, as well.

"You are quiet, Michalis," Helonas observed. "What are you thinking?"

Bolan realized he'd been staring out the window with a blank expression. He yawned and said, "Just dozing, I guess."

"With your eyes open, eh?" Helonas replied with a chuckle.

"Years in prison teaches you to do that," Bolan countered in a friendly tone.

"You appear troubled."

"I'm not sure I can pull this off," Bolan lied, even though he knew a part of what he was saying was the unadulterated truth.

Helonas slapped his leg. "I have faith in you, my brother."

"Yeah. How long will it take us to get to Pátrai?"

"Eight or nine hours," Helonas replied, folding his arms and leaning his head against the chair rest. He closed his eyes before adding, "It is not the distance but the stops that makes it such a long trip."

"Are you sure we have everything we need?"

Helonas opened his eyes now and smiled. "You must learn to trust us, Michalis, no? Just as we must learn to trust you."

"I just want to make sure this goes off okay," Bolan said.

"As do we."

The train suddenly jerked forward and began to shimmy as if it were having a seizure. Even through the heavy windows, Bolan could hear the squeal of brakes. Endre was immediately on his feet and looking out the window. He squinted his dark eyes and then looked harshly at Helonas. He began to speak in Greek, and Bolan only caught a word that he was familiar with now and then.

"What's going on?" Bolan asked.

"Endre thinks it's the police. They have a blockade ahead stopping the train. It is likely they will board and search the entire train."

"We've been blown!" Bolan snarled, jumping from his seat.

He reached inside his jacket and withdrew the Berretta 93-R, setting the selector to 3-round bursts. The other two members—a married couple he knew only as Guilio and Thais—followed his lead and also drew side arms.

"Let us not jump to conclusions," Helonas said calmly. "If we do nothing to alert their suspicions, they will pass us by."

"Maybe," Bolan replied, cracking the door and looking into the narrow corridor. "But what if they find our matériel?"

"That is being shipped out by truck," Helonas said. "You do not think we would arrange to be caught with the goods in hand, do you?"

"And what if Michalis is right, Cyril?" Guilio asked, pointing the muzzle of his Czech-made pistol toward the ceiling. "It is possible someone has set us up."

Bolan saw two men in black fatigues, Kevlar vests and masks round the corner and head directly toward their compartment. He smelled a setup almost immediately, and he was pretty certain these weren't members of the Greek police.

Whoever they were, they moved with the precision of soldiers and experienced combatants, and they clutched Steyr Tactical Machine Pistols. The TMPs were replacements for the MPi models and had become the new standards in production. They had a folding forward handgrip and sound suppressors—there was nothing standard issue about that in the armory of the Greek police.

Two more assailants followed immediately behind them acting as cover.

"Get down!" Bolan yelled as he dived away from the door.

The new arrivals leveled their Steyrs in his direction and blasted the area with 9 mm Parabellum rounds.

The Executioner saw no escape.

There were five of them crammed inside that space. The slugs punching holes and ripping gouges into the walls and door of the cabin seemed endless, and there was little room for them to maneuver when they all heeded Bolan's warning to seek cover. Thais and Guilio cracked heads as they dived to the floor, and one stray round burned a surface wound in Endre's shoulder.

The Executioner needed some room to move.

Bolan looked around a moment and then studied the window. It was long and narrow, but he could squeeze through it and take the heat off the rest of them. If there were guards waiting outside, they would signal to the interior team to break off the engagement and Bolan could draw them away from Helonas and the others.

Then he might be able to escape, which would allow him time to contact Taylor before returning to the group.

Bolan sat up and aimed the Beretta at the window. He squeezed the trigger twice, sweeping the muzzle as he allowed the weapon to cycle through its 3-round bursts. It shattered under the fire, the tinted glass breaking outward and sending sharp missiles whistling through the air.

"What are you doing?" Thais screamed at him.

He flashed her a wicked grin and replied, "Baiting the hunters." Bolan turned to Helonas. "I'm going to draw them away. As soon as I'm gone, you guys can split. Where do you want to meet in Pátrai?"

"I will send Endre with you," Helonas said, shaking his head.

Bolan had to think fast as he jerked his thumb at the big man. "No offense, but I don't think he'll fit through the window."

"Fine, then I will go with you," Helonas replied, grinning and speaking quick instructions to the other three in Greek.

The Executioner just nodded. Helonas's mind was made up and he knew there was very little chance he could change it.

The soldier got to his feet and rushed to the window. He holstered his weapon, then used the cushion to hoist his way up to the frame. He pushed his way through it even as he heard the door opening behind them. Shots rang out, fired by Thais, Guilio and Endre, driving the invaders back as Bolan and Helonas made their escape.

The Executioner dropped to wet ground that sloped from the elevated tracks. He slipped on the grass. His leg buckled under him, and he slid face first down the incline. Helonas followed a moment later, his smaller and more agile form moving a little more gracefully on the slick terrain.

The sounds of gunfire stopped inside the car, and Bolan didn't know whether to assume that meant the rest of them were dead or his ruse had worked. He didn't have long to wait for an answer as he got to his feet and saw six more men, clad in identical attire, bring their machine pistols to bear and charge toward the pair.

"Look out!" Bolan grabbed Helonas's collar and pulled him to the ground as the group opened fire.

The man mumbled some kind of thanks to Bolan because he hadn't seen their attackers.

The Executioner whipped the Beretta into play and shot at the charging group, Parabellum rounds ripping out pieces of rock and earth around the pair as the soldier fired from the prone position. Helonas added to Bolan's fire a moment later, repeatedly squeezing the trigger of the Walther P-38. While his modern version of the Luger wasn't that accurate when fired rapidly, its double-action trigger mechanism facilitated jam-free operation as fast as he could pull the trigger.

Helonas continued the onslaught as Bolan loaded his second clip into the Beretta and thumbed the selector to single shot. As he dropped two of the men with head shots, and Helonas wounded a third with a round through the kneecap, it started to sprinkle. A chilling breeze began to blow, as well, twirling the rain in a cyclonelike pattern and decreasing visibility.

The remaining trio of commandos spread out. They were joined a moment later by four more who jumped from the train. At that distance, the Executioner couldn't tell if it was the same quartet that had attacked them inside, but it didn't matter. It was time to split.

"Let's go," he said to Helonas, jumping to his feet and using the lull in the autofire to rush for the cover of some nearby trees.

Helonas followed him without offering any protest. The terrorist had no idea that the Executioner was experienced in this game of cat-and-mouse. If whoever was after them decided to pursue, they would fan out and try to cover as much area as possible. As soon as they were inside the wood line, Bolan led Helonas on a diagonal course through the thickets and cypress vines. Huge trees cast a seemingly endless canopy of branches above them, with only brief spurts of light from a half moon filtering through it.

Branches and thorny twigs snapped under their weight or left scratches and furrows on their bare skin. The two charged onward in their flight, determined to draw their pursuers into a chase. They were outnumbered and outgunned, trying to lure the commandos from the rest of their team while still attempting to make good on their own escape.

Bolan couldn't help but wonder just who these attackers were. Perhaps they were British—maybe an SAS team that Taylor sent to help him. That didn't make any sense, though, since he hadn't located Hyde-Baker. They wouldn't have pulled him from the mission, and Stony Man would have found a better means of getting him out if they thought his identity was compromised.

But something didn't make sense here because the hit team knew whom to hit and where. They hadn't fired on that compartment by sheer accident. It was a calculated ambush, and only Bolan's ingenuity had saved them from certain death. That would probably score him some points with Helonas and the rest of the group—if they survived—and that would help his cause. Still, the Executioner knew he'd have to find out who these men were one way or another.

Bolan stopped suddenly and Helonas practically tumbled to ground trying to avoid running into him.

"What is wrong?" he asked, his chest heaving.

Bolan wasn't nearly out of breath, and he realized that Helonas wasn't in as good shape as he appeared. Mostly the guy just had muscular arms and chest, but that might have been from weight lifting. Muscle didn't necessarily mean he was well conditioned, and Bolan had spent years under the hardship and endurance required just to stay alive. That wasn't to say he didn't feel the toll it had taken on his physical form.

"I don't want to get too far ahead," Bolan told him. "We have to get them out here, away from our people."

"It wouldn't...surprise me," Helonas puffed, "if they were already dead."

The Executioner threw a surprised look at the man. "I thought you were a team player, Cyril. You don't sound as if you give a damn about the rest of them."

Helonas fixed the soldier with a hot glare. "I care more for those people than you might think, Michalis. Choose your words carefully."

He clapped a hand on Helonas's shoulder and nodded apologetically. "I'm sorry."

"It is forgotten," Helonas said. "Do you—?"

Bolan raised his hand and shook his head, making a shushing noise to quiet the terrorist. The sounds of voices and movement echoed in the silence. Good. The ruse was working and their enemy had taken up the chase. Bolan fired a wild shot in the direction of the noises to let them know they were getting warm.

"Why did you do this?"

"Like I told Thais, it's bait," Bolan said with conviction.

Helonas nodded and the two started away from their pursuers.

And for the second time in less than an hour, Mack Bolan began to work on a plan to ditch Helonas so he could get word to Taylor about the shipment going out by truck. Maybe she could find a way to intercept it. He knew it wasn't going to be easy.

NEMO AMPHIONIDES sat behind his desk and stared at the visitor—the dangerous visitor who was well connected.

As deputy justice minister in the Greek cabinet, Amphionides's own connections spread far and wide. People would have been appalled—if that was even accurate terminology—to know one of the highest law-enforcement officers in Greece was also the father of one of the most wanted criminals in history.

Cyril Helonas Amphionides was more than an anachronism to Amphionides and the rest of his family—he was an embarrassment of the highest order. When his son had announced the decision to join the renegades, Amphionides had done everything to talk him out of it. The 17 November group succeeded because it maintained its anonymity. Amphionides couldn't betray that anonymity because he would, in fact, be turning Judas against his only son. That would never do, despite their disagreements.

Amphionides's bumbling nephew, however, was another story. Midas was barely bright enough to collect his thoughts, a trait that the deputy justice minister knew didn't come from his side of the family. Midas lost his parents at the tender age of twelve, and Amphionides had raised him like one of his own. But the impressionable youth had never quite seemed to recover from the trauma of losing his parents. From the moment he entered their lives, Midas was rebellious and uneducable. He didn't do well at either school or home, and he was always in trouble.

It wasn't any wonder now why the twenty-five-year-old adolescent could barely hold down a job with Pontiki, a job that Amphionides had to blackmail an editor to secure for his nephew no less.

But none of that concerned him nearly as much now as the man that sat before him. He smiled with satisfaction although he could feel a pang of nervousness as he stared into the eyes of Sir Radley Brygmart.

Brygmart was a smart and powerful man who had plenty of connections within the Greek underworld, as well as his own government. He had the power to make Amphionides disappear with a mere word. Not to mention the man's damnable proper attitude got on Amphionides's nerves. Still, the justice minister was quite powerful in his own right, and he tried not to show he was intimidated.

"So, an American agent has penetrated the group," Amphionides said. Brygmart was playing a dangerous game of two ends against the middle here, and Amphionides didn't like it. "What do you plan to do about it?"

"Nothing, for the moment," Brygmart replied quietly. "It was I who allowed the prime minister to alert the Yanks. I saw an opportunity to make them the scapegoat, taking the blame off my government and putting all eyes to America. When the conference fails and Cyril and his people claim responsibility, it can only mean renewed efforts in this ridiculous antiterrorist campaign by NATO."

Amphionides nodded. Despite his uncertainty and distrust of Brygmart, the British secret service agent had a point. A good portion of the money allotted to MI-6 operations in Greece had gone right into their pockets.

Money seemed to be the deciding factor where Brygmart was concerned. It was money that moved lawmakers, bought judges and spawned elections. The Americans had already proved that time and again. But Brygmart's attachment to riches seemed different, somehow. It drove the man but it didn't control him. There was something else he planned to do with his wealth; something bigger and more ambitious, something that surpassed power or prestige.

Amphionides found it very hard to read the intent behind that clever mask, but he knew Brygmart was no fool, either. The guy was biding his time for something.

But what?

"And what of Hyde-Baker?"

Brygmart shrugged. "What of her? Once we have secured the location of the new antiterrorist prototypes, they can dispose of her neatly and quietly. As well as the American."

"Then that leaves only Dina Taylor."

Something cold and hard split Brygmart's normally congenial expression. He shook his head slowly and replied, "You are not to worry about Miss Taylor. I have my own plans for her. She is not to be touched. I never gave you permission to send your men over there. It's a good thing you sent them without identification."

"We're in this together," Amphionides argued. "My neck is on the block here, too, so let's not forget that. I don't need to remind you of the fact Taylor could compromise this whole thing."

"I will take care of it," Brygmart continued in a persistent tone. "Personally."

Amphionides forced a smile. "Come, let us not quibble about this. I will trust you to take care of her. What is your plan in the meantime?"

"We will let the American agent play a free hand in this for a while," Brygmart replied as he inspected his fingernails. "Gain the confidence of the group. I want you to leak it to Cyril that there is a traitor among them, but don't reveal it's the American."

"And how do you propose I do that?"

"Let something slip to Midas," Brygmart replied quickly. "You've always said that he's not very bright. Take him into your confidence. Tell him not to tell Cyril because the time isn't right and you don't want the group distracted from their operations."

Amphionides nodded and said, "So the first thing he'll probably do is run to Cyril and shoot off his mouth. Naturally, they'll be suspicious of the newcomer."

"Exactly," Brygmart replied. "Then we'll put the final stage of our plan into action. At some point the American will make his move. He'll risk rescuing Hyde-Baker, or do something else stupid and then they'll catch him. By that time it will be too late."

"And what if he doesn't reveal himself? What then?"

"Then I will arrange for our people to take him out. You know sooner or later, the undersecretary will crack and reveal the location of the weapons."

"If the American isn't discovered by the time 17 November is ready to steal the L3As, perhaps I will use my men to eliminate him."

Brygmart shook his head. "Why? You've already used them to stop that train."

"To throw him off our scent. We don't want them getting too close and figuring out that we're behind this. Let them think it's the police."

"Fine," Brygmart replied. "It's not worth arguing about."

"I do not understand one thing," Amphionides interjected. "What's in this for you, Sir Brygmart? Why are you cooperating with me in this?"

Brygmart smiled broadly and shook his head. "My dear Deputy Minister, I cannot believe that you would even have to ask me that. You and I both know that the efforts of NATO and Madam Hyde-Baker will never stop 17 November in Greece. The money that I have taken from MI-6 will see better use, believe me. Why should my country pour millions of pounds into a raw deal like this? Such an investment is sacrificial, and benefits neither myself nor Britain."

"So you are doing this for Great Britain?" Amphionides challenged him, knowing the question was a mistake even as he asked it.

"Of course," Brygmart whispered. "The affairs of my nation mean everything to me. I have invested this money in better places and for wiser ends. And you have not suffered from this, either, I might remind you. You have obtained significant gains, both politically and financially, as were your goals. I should think you will probably campaign for prime minister or even president at the coming elections."

Amphionides never ceased to be surprised by Brygmart's observations. The man was astute, intelligent and very wise. Amphionides didn't care what Brygmart had done with the money anyway. He was more concerned with how to eliminate this liability, and he thought he knew how to do it.

He shouldn't have made this bargain; that much was clear now. Brygmart could use his political ambitions against him, and he knew the guy would sell him out if MI-6 discovered the discrepancies and decided to dig deeper. No, Brygmart wasn't the type of man who would go down alone. He'd drag everyone with him, and at this point Amphionides couldn't afford that kind of risk.

When the two men had concluded their business and Brygmart was gone, Amphionides picked up the phone and dialed a special number. It rang twice before it was gruffly answered and Amphionides spoke one word.

"Zeus."

A moment later a second male voice answered, this one quiet with just the hint of a cultured, European accent. Amphionides had never met the man, but he'd used him on numerous occasions. The guy was a tremendous tool when Amphionides needed something taken care of. He was known as a "cleaner," whatever the hell that was, and he was damn good at it.

Blackmail? No problem.

Need someone to disappear? Consider it done.

Arrange an accident? It was just a shame, the tragedies that befell people.

No matter what the job, this man code-named Zeus made

things happen. He'd proved an invaluable tool before and he was now going to prove invaluable again.

"Things are getting out of control here," Amphionides said. The man already knew most of the details, because he'd put him on alert a month earlier. "Once my people have returned, I want both the top dog here eliminated as well as the bitch he's got leashed."

"Fine," the voice said calmly.

"You would like payment arranged in the usual way?"

"Of course."

"It will be done," Amphionides said. He almost broke the connection but then added quickly, "Oh, there might be a third. An American named Belasko."

"An American?" There was a long silence as the man cupped the phone, then returned after speaking with someone for a few moments. "Consider him free of charge."

"Very well," Amphionides replied. "Call me when it's done."

The sunrise shadowed the sky with hues of pink, orange and red as Bolan and Helonas arrived in Pátrai.

Actually, the train hadn't stopped too far from Kórinthos, so the pair managed to board a ferry that took them through the Gulf of Corinth and circled to the north until it arrived in Pátrai.

They had managed to lure their pursuers far enough into the woods that it should have afforded plenty of time for the others to escape. Only time would tell, since they were now within walking distance of the abandoned warehouse designated as the rendezvous point.

Helonas and Bolan had said very little to each other throughout the trip, both of them choosing to concentrate on watching for tails or other suspicious people. They had managed to do this while trying to look inconspicuous themselves.

The Executioner had to admit he was impressed with Cyril Helonas. The terrorist was sharp, and the guy sounded educated and well mannered; he was eloquent and observant, qualities that Bolan hadn't known in many of his enemies. But the man was responsible for countless murders, and his actions were unforgivable as far as Bolan was concerned. Helonas would go down with the rest of the 17 November terrorists, and the soldier wouldn't lose any sleep over it.

They covered the two miles from the wharf to the warehouse in about a half hour. Helonas accessed a back door with a key, and they slipped inside the dusty, metal prefab shell. It was dark and cool, and it looked as if the place had been undisturbed for some time.

Helonas led Bolan to a hallway that branched off the main area and into a small office. The terrorist flipped a switch and the room was bathed in bright light. There was a table with five or six chairs crammed around it, and the Executioner felt somewhat uncomfortable. There was no maneuvering room if things went sour, and he didn't want a repeat performance of what happened in the train car.

"How long have you had this place?" he asked Helonas as he sat at the table.

The Greek criminal smiled as he also took a seat. "It was donated by one of our members, after the government put him out of business. He owed quite a bit of money, and he couldn't repay his loans. Finally his company went under and he owed many governmental taxes. They seized everything, but they did not know that the company that leased this building belonged to us."

Bolan nodded in understanding. "A front."

"Exactly."

"So they turned it back to you thinking that it was rightfully owned by you, and not by him."

"Yes. He deeded the building to us before the government could seize it, as well. Now we take care of him, treat him decently. It is Guilio I speak of. You see, Michalis, that is what 17 November is really about. We take care of one another, and we decide our fate together."

"I see," Bolan observed, "but they still seem to look to you as a sort of leader."

Helonas shook his head. "I provide guidance and logic to our operations. But I am no greater than any of them. There are some much more qualified to speak out, but they choose to remain humble so that they will not risk overpowering anyone else."

"It sounds good in theory," the Executioner pointed out. "But does it really work?"

"It has worked for almost thirty years," Helonas countered with a smile.

"Good point."

There were noises outside the office and the two men drew their pistols simultaneously. A moment later Guilio, Thais and Endre entered, followed by two more members from the group. Bolan didn't know the names of the other two yet, but he knew they would all comprise the inside team under his direction.

Helonas put his weapon away and rose to greet the group, hugging and kissing each one in turn. Bolan just nodded, choosing to forgo the traditional greetings. He did shake Guilio's hand, and Thais planted a peck on his cheek, which surprised the soldier. They were slowly beginning to accept him into the group.

When the rounds of greetings and such were finished, the group huddled around the table and Helonas brought out the map he'd first shown Bolan in Athens. He spread the diagrams on the table and called for everyone to be silent.

"Before I let Michalis hand out the assignments," he began, "I want each of you to know how proud I am to work with you. You are my friends, my family. I trust that the gods will go with us on this journey."

They all nodded and became silent for a moment. No heads were bowed, no eyes were closed, but it seemed as if they were offering up some kind of prayer. Bolan began to feel uncomfortable as the silence weighed heavily in the room. After nearly a minute, they all returned to a normal state and Helonas nodded to him.

Bolan took his cue and directed everyone to the map. "We now have enough explosives to break through the structural supports here, here and here. That will be in the subbasement. I'm guessing we'll need to plant about three hundred pounds of ammonium nitrate shaped charges in order to weaken the structure." He looked at Endre. "You're sure we got everything on that list?"

Endre nodded.

"Good," Bolan retorted.

Thais raised her hand, then said, "Three hundred pounds is quite a bit."

Helonas nodded his agreement. "Not to mention the plastique."

"We'll have to go in two teams," Bolan said. "It's the only way we can make this happen. Cyril and two others on the first run with the ammonium nitrate, Endre, Guilio and myself in the second team. We'll detonate the ammonium nitrate from the inside, then blow the C-4 on the way out to crack the seams on the ground and first sublevel. That should be enough to allow weight and gravity to do the rest."

"What about security?" Guilio interjected.

Bolan looked at each member in turn as he spoke. "According to the intelligence from Cyril, the front entrance is out of the question. There are two guards in the back, and a couple of cleaning crews apparently show up every night. We're going to commandeer their vehicle and uniforms to get us inside."

"And if we cannot?" Endre queried.

"Then we'll kill them," Helonas replied with a cool menace before the Executioner could conjure a more reasonable reply.

"We don't want to draw attention to ourselves, Cyril," Bolan warned the terrorist.

"Once we have the explosives planted, it won't really matter, will it?"

The group let out grunts and nods of agreement, and Bolan had no choice but play along.

"Now," Helonas continued, "let's get some rest. The operation begins in a few hours and it has been a long night for all of us."

THE GOVERNMENT BUILDING SAT on a quiet, private thoroughfare in midtown Pátrai. At any given time throughout the day, there were two to three hundred staff, dignitaries and assistants to members of the PM's cabinet working inside the offices housed within the huge building.

And that's what concerned Dina Taylor the most. How in the hell was she going to evacuate all of those people without alerting 17 November that it wasn't just business as usual?

Evening drew near as Taylor parked her car in the visitors' lot and made her way to the entrance. She'd left her pistol behind, knowing she'd never get past the metal detector. Actually, she'd used some connections within MI-6 who worked in the building to get her an appointment with the head of building security.

With an appointment, it wasn't difficult to get past the guards and soon she found herself on the fifth floor. Before long she was inside the office and seated in front of the security adviser, crammed in there with three other advisers.

All of them were looking at her as if she'd come down from bloody Saturn or something to rain on their parade. The whole thing was getting damn ugly, and she tried not to raise her voice as she attempted to explain the gravity of the situation to these narrow-minded simpletons. It didn't seem to be doing her much good.

"I know you think I'm some kind of flake, Mr. Stapol," she stated, "but whether you like it or not, within an hour or two members of 17 November are going to level this building."

"You must understand how this looks, Miss Crysanthos."

Taylor shook her head. "No, but I'm sure you're going to tell me. Aren't you?"

"You have no idea what you are asking," he said, rising from his chair and coming around his desk. He held out his hand and gestured for her to stand. He then escorted her to the door, adding, "I will be happy to look into what you have told me, but I see no reason to clear everyone from this building unless you can bring me some proof."

"I have proof, you bloody dimwit!" Taylor argued, pulling herself from his grasp and stamping her foot. "I'm the one who supplied the explosives to these people. They ordered three hundred pounds of ammonium nitrate and about forty detonators. Aren't you listening? They are the same ones who kidnapped Undersecretary Hyde-Baker!"

Stapol sighed and gestured to his men, who surrounded Taylor as he stepped out of the way. "I will follow up with my people and double the guards this evening."

As the men crowded Taylor toward the door of the office she asked, "Would it make any difference if I told you I work for the British government?"

"None whatsoever," he called after her. "Good day, Miss Crysanthos."

Moments later Taylor found herself standing outside the office as the door was slammed in her face.

She whirled and stormed toward the elevators, heartbeat thudding in her ears as she fumed over the situation. Oddly enough, she hadn't been able to get in touch with Sir Brygmart and now she couldn't even get the Greek government officials to listen.

It hadn't been the first time since she came to Greece. It seemed that most of the Greeks wanted to turn a deaf ear when anyone mentioned 17 November. It sounded so innocent but she wasn't fooled by such semantics. There was an ominous tone behind it and it seemed that even talk of the terrorist organization was like a thorn in the flesh of the country and its people.

Particularly the bureaucrats. This was getting out of control, and if she didn't think of something, a lot of people would die. But Taylor knew she had to grasp the reality of the situation, and that meant she had to begin with the fact she couldn't get the innocent civilians out of the building by conventional means.

She would have to think of something else. And right at that moment, she couldn't help but wonder about the circumstances of a certain dark-haired, blue-eyed stranger and what he was doing right at that moment.

MACK BOLAN ZIPPED into the maintenance worker's orange coveralls and hoped nobody would notice it was almost two sizes too small. But it was the biggest one they had.

They had decided to put Endre and Helonas in suits, and a connection in Pátrai had quickly forged some company credentials that identified them as company inspectors. They all had new documents that they could present with the proper stamps and security clearances. For all intents and purposes, they wouldn't have any trouble getting past the pair of lax guards who probably saw that same van and those bright suits day in and day out.

The Executioner had inspected the explosives brought by the two nameless men who'd accompanied the others at the warehouse. No one had bothered to really introduce the men, although Bolan now knew their first names.

Jason and Mette watched him with a fair amount of distrust registering in their faces, and the soldier couldn't help feeling some apprehension of his own as a result. He chose to ignore them, though, and finished dressing and began to inspect the large cleaning machines they would use to smuggle the shape charges inside.

"Much like the Trojan horse, no?" Helonas asked Bolan as they jounced along in the truck, throwing them into the unforgiving metal walls.

The government of Pátrai apparently hadn't learned how to keep its roads in good repair.

"It's going to make a hell of a bang," the Executioner replied with a grin.

"How long will it take us to set those up?" Mette asked, nodding at the shaped charges.

It was the first time he'd spoken to Bolan.

"They're already primed," the Executioner assured him. "All you have to do is make sure you put them where I told you. Simple physics will do the rest, and Cyril will make sure there's no mistakes."

"Don't worry, Mette," Helonas chided him. "Michalis knows what he is doing."

That seemed to satisfy both of the men. They were much younger than the other members of the group, barely college age. They seemed to look up to Cyril and trust him. Perhaps they had been students and Helonas had recruited them. It seemed the principles behind the acceptance process in the group followed a similar course to those of gangs and cults in America.

The penniless, homeless and any other dregs of society without direction could find security and warmth—a place to share and grow. It was simply a matter of supplying the basic human need of acceptance. It was about getting people to trust and then manipulating that to further personal or financial ends. In the long run, as long as those individuals got whatever it was they needed from the group, it didn't matter to what levels they might have to succumb, or what injustices and perversions they might suffer.

It was actually the worst kind of exploitation imaginable to Bolan, because it usually victimized the innocent first. Well, the Executioner could see what was really going on and he knew how to deal with it. The basic tenets of Animal Man hadn't changed over the years, and one of those rules was survival of the fittest.

Mack Bolan had chosen to represent those who couldn't fight for themselves a long time ago. Throughout his war against the irredeemable enemies of humankind—the Mafia, the KGB, terrorists—Bolan had always taken the war to them. He'd fought them on his terms, not theirs, and they had always cowered under the blitzing fire. It simply proved one thing: they were bullies and cowards, and as such they would cringe every time they met up with someone who was willing to fight back.

The principle was simple. It was the execution that was quite another matter.

The van ground to a halt with a long squeal of brakes, and the back doors opened a moment later. Thais leaned inside and whispered something to Helonas in Greek. The terrorist nodded and then gestured for Jason and Mette to each take a machine.

"I will follow you," Helonas told them as they prepared to disembark from the truck. "Do not speak to the guards unless directly spoken to. I will do the talking."

The men nodded and then jumped out. Bolan slid the large cleaning machines to them. He pulled Helonas up short and threw him a warning look. "You only have about twenty minutes once the charges are set. So plant them and get out."

"Do not worry, my friend," Helonas said, patting Bolan's shoulder. "We shall be in and out before you know it."

The Executioner nodded and watched them depart. A moment later, Thais closed the doors. The truck rumbled to life and pulled away from the back entrance. The plan called for both teams to get inside the building at the same time. There was no way they could get four past the guards at once, since that would have seemed odd, so they decided to try a very old ploy.

Thais drove the truck to a point about five miles from the building. She picked up Endre and Guilio, and the trio rode in back for the return to their target. It would appear that she had made a second trip to get them, which was apparently the normal routine for the cleaning company.

As they rode, Bolan thought of the poor technicians bound and gagged at the warehouse. The terrorists had seen no need to kill the men, since they were just common workers. It was odd for an organization like 17 November not to murder freely, but they apparently didn't feel that way. Their targets were the diplomats and businessmen, those who allegedly threatened a free and independent Greece.

The truck halted again, and once again Thais opened the doors to allow them to exit. Bolan grabbed the two jugs, which normally contained cleaning solution, and Guilio snagged the final machine. The two bailed out with Endre and marched purposefully toward the back entrance.

Endre nodded to the guards, and the trio produced their papers. One of the guards checked each document in turn and then returned them to the men. He then nodded to his colleague, who turned, punched in a code number on the twelve-character keypad and then opened the door to allow them to pass.

Bolan shook his head after they were inside and leaned close to Guilio's ear. "That was easier than I thought."

The Greek only nodded but a cruel smile played across his lips. The men walked directly to the service elevator and Endre stabbed the call button. They waited patiently, looking around with disinterested expressions. The place seemed completely deserted.

Suddenly, there was a buzzing sound as a door in a bank of elevators down the hallway opened. A group of men and women walked out and casually strolled toward the front entrance. The Executioner froze and felt his stomach leap into his throat.

There were still people in the building!

Either Taylor hadn't been able to evacuate the place or she hadn't understood his cryptic message at the meet. In any case, it meant Bolan was out of options. He couldn't risk blowing the place up and killing an unknown number of innocent people. He needed to formulate a new plan and quickly.

But the sudden sound of an alarm changed everything in a split second. Bolan heard shouts coming from the front of the building. A moment later, Taylor rounded a corner with gun in hand. The crazy MI-6 agent charged the trio, leveling the muzzle of her weapon in Bolan's direction and screaming something at the top of her lungs.

Bolan reached inside his coveralls for the Beretta 93-R as the madwoman opened fire.

Endre was the first one to fall under Taylor's brash assault.

She squeezed the trigger of her Walther PPK rapidly, snapping off three rounds toward the towering Greek. The 9 mm short slugs dotted his chest as he reached for his pistol, continuing through his tender flesh until they perforated the lungs. The giant terrorist took several uncertain, wheezing breaths before toppling backward.

Bolan aimed high and fired once, making sure the shot would go nowhere near Taylor. Guilio reached into the pocket of the coveralls for his own pistol, a 9 mm Zastava M-88. He fired at Taylor wildly, his shots zipping around her as he tried to gain target acquisition. Taylor continued to move toward them in a zigzag pattern.

The Executioner waited until Guilio's attention was on her lithe form before turning the Beretta in his direction and squeezing off a 3-round burst. The 9 mm subsonic rounds punched gaping holes in the terrorist's side as he was lifted off his feet by the impact. Guilio's corpse slammed into the wall near the elevator door and slid to the floor. Pink, frothy bubbles issued from his nose and mouth.

The elevator door opened just as Taylor reached Bolan. The Executioner grabbed Endre by the collar and gestured for her to cover him. He dragged the big man into the elevator, ducking as she fired shots at the security men who kept peering around the corner. He dragged Guilio in next, then pushed the machines inside before gesturing for Taylor to follow.

The MI-6 agent popped off two more shots before joining him. She loaded a spare clip as Bolan stabbed the button that would take them to the floor below.

Taylor smiled as she struggled to catch her breath. "I thought that would get your attention."

"We're not out of the woods yet," Bolan told her. "There's another group in the subbasement, planting those shaped charges. You've got to get everybody out of here."

"You mean you actually intend to blow the place?" Taylor asked with disbelief in her voice.

"Of course not," Bolan said as the doors opened on the basement. "I've arranged for them to put those charges where they'll do the least damage, not the most."

"Then if these people aren't in any danger, why are you trying to get them out?" Taylor argued.

She stood over him as he dropped to one knee and uncapped one of the cleaning machines. The basement was dank and musty from years of disuse. Pillars along several key points, as well as a stem wall supported it. Bolan looked up and figured the ceiling clearance at about eight or nine feet. It was actually one big, open room and the soldier was thankful for that. It would make it a hell of a lot easier to minimize damage if the concussion from the C-4 had some place to go.

As he began to pull blocks of C-4 from inside the machine, Taylor added, "There isn't time to clear everybody out of here!"

Bolan stopped what he was doing and looked up at her. "There's time if you stop standing here arguing with me and go do it."

"Look, Yank, I've already talked to the head of security. He doesn't believe me. He thinks the whole thing is a hoax and I'm some kind of flake."

Bolan got to his feet, looked around and saw the small device he was looking for near the elevator. He walked over to it, smashed the glass with his fist and pulled the lever. The fire Klaxons began to sound throughout the building, nearly deafening the pair as they echoed through the long, low confines of the basement.

"What the hell are you doing?" Taylor demanded.

"Solving your problem. Now I've helped you do your job, you help me do mine."

Taylor put her hands on her hips, studied him a moment, made a face as if to say something and then began to laugh. Finally, she bent down and began helping the Executioner pull out the blocks of C-4 as he primed each one of them with the detonators she'd provided.

Bolan looked at his watch. There were ten minutes left before they had to be out of there, right along with everyone else. The soldier could only hope the innocents got out alive.

But another problem had now presented itself. While Bolan could explain the deaths of Endre and Guilio easily enough, security officers for the complex would now be looking for them, as well. If they ran into Helonas and his crew while searching for Taylor, things could get ugly. The Executioner couldn't live with the thought of leaving the security people to perish at the hands of a man like Helonas.

"I need you to create a diversion," Bolan told her.

"What?"

"I need you to find security," he replied, "but make them think they found you. Tell them you started a fire and you're going to burn the place down."

"Have you lost your bloody mind, Yank?"

"No," he countered, "but apparently they think you have. They'll have to believe the fire is real, and they won't cancel the evacuation. When you see the security chief, tell him what's really going on and keep everybody away long enough for me to finish the job."

"Why the facade, Belasko?" she asked. "I don't understand."

"I don't have time to explain it now," Bolan said, piling the C-4 in the center of the room. "You're just going to have to trust me. Now beat it."

"All right, I'll trust you. But you watch your ass."

Bolan grunted with a nod. He checked his watch again before completing his task. Yeah, putting the explosives in the center of the room would cause very little damage. At the worst, it would blow a hole in the floor. Most of the damage would be contained to this room, and nothing that some plastering and refinishing wouldn't take care of.

The numbers began to count down in his head. Helonas had three more minutes before he had to be out of there and head to the first floor. They could go out the back, make it look just like they were evacuating with everyone else. Then the Executioner could do his thing, and watch the surprise on Helonas's face when their plans went right down the tubes.

The fire alarm clanged incessantly, and the loud echo was beginning to give the Executioner a headache.

As the minutes ticked by, the alarms within the complex fell silent. Apparently someone had keyed the switch to turn them off. He listened closely for the sounds of movement above but he heard nothing above the ringing in his ears.

He stood and walked to a stairwell on the far side of the basement, quickly ascending them two at a time. He reached the ground landing and trotted in the direction of the back door. He passed the main elevator bank in time to see one set of doors open and Helonas emerge with Jason and Mette.

"Good timing," Bolan murmured as Helonas fell into step.

"Where are Guilio and Endre?" the terrorist asked.

"Dead."

"What?"

Bolan shook his head, looking around as he kept his voice low. "We got surprised by security people. They drew down on us and took them out. I managed to lose them, but I had to plant the charges on my own. Endre and Guilio didn't make it."

The soldier clammed up as they reached the back door. The four men exited quickly. The guards waved at their truck, yelling for them to hurry and get away from the building. The four jumped into the back, and Helonas smiled reassuringly at the senior of the pair. The man threw him a quick salute and then closed the back doors. Helonas leaned forward and ordered Thais to go, then turned to Bolan with an expectant look.

"I don't understand this," he said with an unmistakable edge in his tone. "You manage to escape but Endre and Guilio are dead?"

"Somebody is on to us, Cyril," Bolan replied, raising his hands in defense. "First we get blown on the train, now someone sets a trap for us here."

"Or perhaps for you," Jason suggested.

Bolan suddenly looked at the control panel on the floor. "Tell Thais to stop. Now!"

He reached for the radio panel wired to detonate the charges. He flipped the main switch, but Helonas grabbed the panel from him before he could do anything else. Bolan looked at him in surprise and was ready to offer protest, but he noticed Jason was now covering him with a pistol. Bolan shook his head and looked at Helonas with genuine anger.

"You think I'm a traitor?" Bolan snapped.

"I'm not sure," Helonas said, the trepidation obvious in his voice. "But I do not wish to take any chances. I will make sure this goes right."

The men waited as Helonas climbed down from the truck and flipped the four switches below the main primer in succession. There was only a small boom as the sublevel explosives ignited, and Bolan watched Helonas's face carefully for any reaction. The normally joyful, smug expression fell to a mask of disappointment as the echo of the blasts died.

Bolan had to fight back the urge to grin. Helonas had planted enough shaped charges to bring the foundation in on itself. What he didn't know was that the charges were actually the cratering type. They were used to blow holes in the ground, and that's exactly what they had done. They were absolutely no threat to the support pillars.

Helonas climbed into the back of the truck, closed the doors behind him and ordered Thais to continue. Jason hadn't lowered his pistol and Helonas sat near Bolan, staring at him suspiciously.

"It didn't work, Michalis," he said quietly.

Bolan kept his face impassive. "I'm sorry, Cyril. I did my best."

"Perhaps. And perhaps someone is on to us."

"Or on to you," Jason added, jabbing the pistol in Bolan's face.

Helonas raised his hand and ordered Jason to stop. "Put the gun away. We do not treat each other like this."

"But we hardly know him, Cyril."

Helonas looked at the Executioner before turning back to glare at Jason. "But I think I know him well enough. He wouldn't have gone this far just to betray us. It wouldn't make any sense. He got the explosives and he planned the entire operation. And he did it in front of Endre. There is no way he could have planned all of that to fail. There was no opportunity. Now put the gun away, Jason."

The young man obeyed although he was obviously anxious to kill the Executioner. He was as brainwashed as the rest of the group. Bolan could see the hate and terrorist fervor burning behind those young, innocent eyes. He recognized it because he'd seen it thousands of times before. Many times he'd seen it right before squeezing the trigger.

Jason and Mette were examples of just one of the many evils of terrorism. It took young, impressionable people who might otherwise lead a valuable, upright existence and corrupted their views to suit evil ambitions. Bolan couldn't even begin to count the number of youngsters he'd encountered who had succumbed to such lunacy. It angered him every time he thought about it, and he found a renewed distaste for people like Helonas.

"You cannot be trusted completely yet," Helonas told Bolan, "but I do not believe you had anything to do with the deaths of Guilio and Endre. Your actions at the train saved this operation and us. Based on that alone, I choose to give you the benefit of the doubt. I'm sure the rest of the group will agree."

"I just didn't have time to plant those charges correctly without help," Bolan replied.

"I know," Helonas assured him. "Let us put the matter behind us."

The Executioner inclined his head in the direction of the truck cab. "What will you tell Thais?"

"I am not sure yet," Helonas whispered, "but I'm sure she will understand. We all know the risks."

Bolan wondered if they truly did.

THE GROUP DECIDED to leave Pátrai that night and return to Athens by bus. It seemed the most likely method of transportation that would allow them to escape detection. Just to make sure, Thais left on the first bus with Jason and Mette, and Helonas and Bolan took another bus that was headed to Athens by a more indirect route.

Helonas obviously wanted to keep his eye on the Executioner. Either that or he really liked the American but wasn't about to admit it.

The Greek terrorist had kept Jason from putting a bullet in Bolan's head, and that was something the soldier didn't take lightly. Perhaps the group had already lost two good members, and their size couldn't permit a third loss. Moreover, the rest of them had obviously decided Bolan was to stay unharmed.

Thais didn't seem to hold the death of her husband against him, and that probably surprised him more than anybody. The "failure" in Pátrai had created the desired effect and elicited the right responses from 17 November. Bolan was now fairly certain he knew how to destroy the group, using their obvious weaknesses against them without their knowing it.

Perhaps he could take a less direct approach, just as he had when working against the Mafia. Bolan had found role camouflage an invaluable weapon against terrorist groups like this one. They prided themselves so much on their closeness that their very aversions to strangers and outsiders repeatedly proved their undoing. Once they decided to trust someone, they decided to trust them fully. It was this weakness that made the Executioner's job easy.

The two men were now seated in the very back of the bus.

It wasn't that crowded, since bus tickets were rather expensive. Traveling by bus wasn't common under the same principles of automobile ownership. It was reserved for middle class and those with the extra money to travel by such means.

Most of the riders were seated toward the front of the bus so it was easy to talk quietly among themselves without being overheard.

"I want to discuss our plans for the next operation," Helonas said. "You and I will play key roles in this one."

"What's the target?"

Helonas shook his head and grinned. "No target this time. At least not one we're going to blow up. This time, my friend, we're going to steal something."

"I don't understand."

"Have you ever heard of the L3A?"

Bolan pretended to think hard for a moment and then shook his head. Of course, he actually did know something of it. John "Cowboy" Kissinger had first briefed Stony Man on it, and Bolan got a couple of details by Carl Lyons later during a mission with Able Team.

While he didn't know a lot about it, he knew the L3A design was based on the Stoner SR-25. It was under very secretive design and testing specifications but Bolan knew the prototypes had recently been completed, and the weapon was soon to be announced as the high-tech solution to antiterrorist units around the world.

"It is rumored to be a fantastic new rifle," Helonas whispered excitedly. "It was designed by a British company, and my sources tell me that one thousand prototypes were delivered to some location in Great Britain."

"Some location?" Bolan echoed. "England's a big place. Any idea where to start looking?"

"No, but it is only a matter of time."

"What do you mean?"

"You know of the disappearance of Undersecretary Hyde-Baker?"

"Yeah."

"We have her as a prisoner at our base in Athens," Helonas said. "I have not yet pulled the location from her. Her resistance to legitimate questioning is considerable, and I might have to apply more conventional means to get her to cooperate with us."

So that was it. They had kidnapped Hyde-Baker for the purpose of locating the new L3A. Bolan saw an advantage, and he decided to lower the bait into the water and see if his fish bit.

"Maybe you should let me take a crack at her," Bolan suggested.

"Really?" Helonas said, seemingly interested now.

"Yeah. I learned quite a few things from the South Americans in prison. I'm sure I could have her chattering like a squirrel in no time."

"I don't know."

"Well, if you really don't trust me, then maybe you'd better not."

Helonas's face darkened a shade. "I never said I didn't trust you. I'm just being careful is all. Perhaps I will afford you the opportunity to question her."

"Fine. So what's the big deal about this L3A?"

"We could use such advanced equipment to further our own goals." Helonas looked around to make sure nobody was listening, then lowered his voice even more and leaned toward Bolan. "There's a meeting scheduled between major members of our government and NATO in three days. My sources tell me that someone plans to testify against certain members of the Greek cabinet who support our cause. We cannot, of course, allow this."

"It sounds personal," Bolan said.

Helonas nodded. "In some ways it is, my friend. But in either case we cannot allow this mysterious individual to testify. I plan to steal these weapons so that we might stop the conference and make a statement to those who interfere with our people."

"You know what security is going to be like?"

"Of course," he said with a shrug. "But if this L3A can do

what it is rumored to be able to do, we shall not have a problem."

Bolan couldn't argue with that. Technology was a great thing when it was applied by the right people. Nonetheless, when it fell into the hands of terrorists, it could be a scourge. It didn't matter if it was as small as a computer chip or as large a missile. Whatever good people could find in new technology, others could find a way to use it for just as evil a purpose.

"It sounds as if you're planning the mission to end all missions."

"Oh no, Michalis," Helonas replied with a cruel smile. "This is only the beginning."

Stony Man Farm, Virginia

Hal Brognola paced the War Room like an expectant father, grinding an unlit cigar between his teeth. The Stony Man chief kept glancing at the large digital clock on the wall. Dammit, where the hell was McCarter?

Things had gone downhill since Bolan's departure for Greece. Intelligence reports made it appear as if the man had just disappeared off the face of the planet, but Brognola had learned to put little weight in those reports. Nonetheless, even Aaron Kurtzman was having trouble locating him.

And then there was this latest news from Dina Taylor's superiors. The only thing they could confirm was that Bolan had gotten inside the group, but beyond that they supposedly knew nothing. Now they claimed they couldn't even find Taylor. Moreover, Barbara Price's intelligence connections indicated Taylor might have gone AWOL on them. That would put the Executioner in a precarious situation if that were more than just a rumor.

Bolan hadn't wanted to work with MI-6 on this one, and he'd made it clear before taking the mission. But personal preference wasn't always the motivation in the warrior's agenda.

Brognola had known Mack "the Bastard" Bolan for many years, although it seemed as if nothing had really changed between them. Sure, they'd been through some tough times since then. Hell, Brognola owed his life and the lives of his family members to the warrior. It was a debt he could never repay, yet it was one the Executioner had never tried to collect.

In fact, Bolan had never mentioned it again after the incident with Nicky Gianelli and Cameron Cartwright. Two men—one a mobster and the other a member of the CIA—had kidnapped Brognola's family and tried to destroy the Stony Man chief. They hadn't counted on Mack Bolan entering the fray, and when all was said and done Brognola got his life and his family back. Yes, it was a blood debt.

Since that time, numerous offers had been made to bring the Executioner back into the fold, but it just wasn't in the cards. The soldier preferred a lone-wolf status. Perhaps there was so much blood on his hands, so many ghosts from the past, that wouldn't allow him to drag others down the same path.

And perhaps Harold Brognola—despite his enduring friendship with the man they called the Executioner—would never know for certain. Partly because Mack Bolan was a tough act to follow. Just when Brognola thought he had the man figured out, Bolan did something to turn the tables. The guy was always thinking on his feet; he was always in forward motion with some new strategy for success.

His ability to make war against the cannibals of society, coupled with his consummate soldiering, caused the enemy to scuttle into the corners like roaches frightened of the light. Mack Bolan brought justice where there was lawlessness, hope to the hopeless and fear to the hearts of the arrogant.

And if he was in trouble, Brognola would pull out all of the stops to help him.

David McCarter walked through the door of the War Room, a cigarette in one hand and a can of Coca-Cola Classic in the other. The Briton veteran smiled at Brognola, dimples cracking the foxlike features. McCarter was as tough as they came. He was a warrior who loved the thrill of combat, although he'd outgrown some of his more hard-charging, act-without-thinking ways as the years had gone by. But that hadn't made him any less effective. He was still a crack pistol marksman and a valued member of Phoenix Force.

"Sorry, Hal," he said, dropping into a chair. "I got here as soon as I could. What's up?"

"I wish I could say," Brognola said, taking a seat. "We got word from some high-ups in MI-6 that Striker seems to have disappeared."

"What do you mean 'disappeared'?" McCarter replied, stiffening in his chair. Something changed in his expression and Brognola knew he had the man's attention. "People don't just disappear, Hal."

"I realize that. Aaron's been keeping an eye out for any new information. I called you here because of Dina Taylor. I want to know if there's anything else you can tell me about her."

McCarter shrugged. "After talking to Barbara, I figured you had more information than I did. I haven't talked to her in years."

"Okay, but is she reliable?"

"In what sense?"

"In the strictest sense. What I want to know is if you think she'd ever turn traitor."

"Taylor?" McCarter snorted and shook his head. "Not in a million years. That's one hard-core patriot there, Hal. If she committed to helping Mack or finding Hyde-Baker, she'd bloody well make good on it. Taylor's like me in many respects. Strictly do-or-die all the way. I couldn't believe she'd go sour."

"Well, that's the word I'm getting from her own people, and since you know her better than I do, I figured you could help us predict where this is going and what we should do next."

McCarter nodded emphatically and replied, "I'll do everything I can."

Kurtzman and Price entered the briefing area a moment later. The computer whiz's expression would have suggested there was some kind of update, and a grin pasted to the big man's face made Brognola relax considerably.

At least the Executioner was alive.

The Stony Man leader had forgone the idea of sending Jack Grimaldi to Athens until they had some information and came up with a safe plan for the two men to make contact. If Striker had managed to penetrate 17 November, it was a fair bet he was eventually going to need Grimaldi's support. The ace flier factored heavily into Bolan's plans. That was one of the things that made Bolan successful in what he did. The soldier knew how to utilize the Stony Man resources to their maximum potential.

Kurtzman rolled himself up to the table as Price rubbed McCarter's shoulder in way of greeting and then took a seat next to him.

"What do we know?" Brognola asked.

"Quite a bit more than we did this morning," Price said enthusiastically. She nodded to Kurtzman to indicate he should begin the briefing.

"We received word of some activity in Pátrai. We're not absolutely sure of all the details, but we know for certain that Mack was involved and that it was 17 November behind the attack."

"And how do we know this?" Brognola interjected with a quizzical expression.

"Two reasons," Price answered. "One, they claimed credit for the attack. Two, we have it through official channels that Dina Taylor tried to warn security in the building about the impending attack. She couldn't have known about it unless Mack found some way to tell her."

"What did they do?" McCarter asked.

"Tried to blow up a political building," Kurtzman replied. "It was a satellite office for members of the presidential cabinet. Most of the people working there are either deputies or aides to the cabinet members, but the high-level diplomats visit occasionally, and it is frequented by parliament members who represent the northern areas of the country."

"Anybody get hurt?"

"Two fatalities. Cleanup crews near the explosion area discovered the remains. Greek authorities have had trouble identifying them because there apparently wasn't much left. Initial data would suggest they might have been members of 17 November who got caught in the blast. Everyone else who has clearance or works in the building has been accounted for."

"Sounds like 17 November blew it," McCarter observed.

"Sounds like Striker's handiwork," Brognola suggested. "Maybe these two got caught up in the blast by design. Do we know why the bombs didn't work?"

"No," Kurtzman retorted, shaking his head, "but Barbara's got her intelligence connections working on that as we speak. There were other interests in that building, as well, not to mention this was a terrorist action, so Greece is cooperating with both British and American intelligence agents in the investigation. We should have some solid answers within the hour."

"Good enough," Brognola said.

He turned to Price. "You said that Taylor tried to warn officials about the attack?"

"Yes, she was questioned several hours by the chief of security before being released to MI-6."

It felt like a rock hit the pit of Brognola's stomach. "Something's wrong here," he said sternly, his eyes resting on McCarter with purpose. "I just talked to MI-6 and they're giving me a completely different story. They said that Taylor's gone rogue and they have no idea what's going on."

"That's what they'd like us to think," the Phoenix Force veteran retorted. "Did I misunderstand something? I thought this request for help came from the office of the British prime minister."

"It did," Price said.

"Then I'm thinking that someone inside the British government is as dirty as they come."

"Striker wondered the same thing," Brognola admitted, "after we told him that 17 November knew about Madam Hyde-Baker's visit to Thessaloníki. For some reason, they want us to believe that Taylor is working independently of them or Striker."

"That doesn't make any sense," McCarter said. "We sent him

to help them get Hyde-Baker back. It was Dina who made the contacts to start with."

"I know, David," Brognola said. "Which brings me to another question. What reason did 17 November have to kidnap the undersecretary? There's been no ransom demand and no operations in Greece that we could connect her to directly."

"Other than their desire to stifle the conference between Greek officials and NATO," Price reminded him.

Brognola shook his head and frowned. "I don't buy that. Not completely, anyway. There has to be something else going on here. There's no logic in 17 November's actions. They're an organized and highly effective group. We're missing something."

"What about the L3A?" McCarter suggested after a long time of silence.

"What?" Brognola said blankly, not really understanding the reference. His concerns for Bolan in conjunction with trying to clear up the mystery now before them had him preoccupied.

Price's expression revealed her surprise. "Oh, of course! David could be right, Hal. It's so obvious that we never thought of it before."

"What are you talking about?" Brognola asked.

"Remember the L3A? The new antiterrorist weapon Cowboy briefed us about two or three months ago?"

"Of course," Brognola said, remembering the meeting clearly now. Then it dawned on him and he realized where they were going with this. "You think they snatched Hyde-Baker to get their hands on the L3A?"

"Why not?" Price said shrugging. "It makes perfect sense now. The L3A was specifically commissioned for testing and manufacture as part of the Sheringham Articles. Hyde-Baker was the chief architect of that program, and she helped them get the allocations and such pushed through the British parliament."

"What do we know about this thing?" Brognola asked, turning toward Kurtzman.

Kurtzman saw his cue and went to a nearby computer terminal. He projected an image of weapons schematics up on the screen and dimmed the lights. The other three turned their attention toward the screen as Kurtzman engaged an interactive program he'd designed around the schematics.

"This is the information we've gleaned from Stony Man's sources. British engineer Bradley Marshfield created the original design. It was licensed for manufacture and prototype testing by Royal Arms of India."

"It's based on the Stoner SR-25, right?" McCarter interrupted.

"You bet," Kurtzman replied. He tapped a key and a close-up of the weapon appeared. "It's carbine style and hailed as the only electrically powered SMG in the world. It has a folding stock, and the fore grip contains six 5.2-volt nickel-metal hydride batteries to power the firing, extraction and sighting systems. It's capable of emptying a 60-round magazine in about four seconds."

McCarter whistled. "Boy, we would all like to get our hands on one of those."

"That's not all," Kurtzman continued. "It also fires a rip-off design from the Russian 7.63 mm SP round."

Brognola furrowed his eyebrows. "SP?"

It was McCarter who answered him. "Stands for 'silent pistol,' except that in this case the cartridge is slightly longer than a pistol casing. I've only heard rumors, but the bullet is apparently nothing more than standard M-1943 ball ammunition."

"Does it work like the subsonic cartridges we use?" Brognola asked.

"Not exactly," Kurtzman replied. "In this case, there's a piston located inside the cartridge between the powder and the bullet itself. When the primer ignites the powder, the piston pushes the round out but seals in all the gas, and thus the explosion."

"And abracadabra," McCarter concluded, "no noise."

"It doesn't break any records in the speed department," Kurtzman added, "but it doesn't have to. It can propel many rounds a short distance with accuracy and silence, and those are features that come in handy in close-quarters combat and antiterrorist actions."

"Amen to that, blokes," McCarter agreed quietly.

"You said it's electrically charged?" Brognola echoed.

"Yes," Kurtzman said. "There are three spares attached to the stock. The batteries also facilitate a feature that allows the scope signature to change from infrared to sighting for small-arms demolitions."

McCarter tossed Kurtzman a surprised look in the dim lights. "The bloody thing comes with a grenade launcher?"

"Oh, yeah," he replied matter-of-factly. "Standard 40 mm designed to fire the PTFE, and Argus grenades manufactured by the Swiss."

Brognola shook his head with disbelief as Kurtzman discontinued the images and raised the lights.

An unusual quiet settled over the room. Each of the Stony Man members was lost in his or her thoughts, obviously considering the gravity of what Kurtzman had told them. The entire operation confounded Brognola, and he found himself speechless for the first time in quite a while.

He considered the best course of action might be none at all. The Stony Man chief certainly didn't want to do anything that might compromise the Executioner's cover. Obviously, someone inside 17 November trusted him because he had somehow managed to thwart their attempts to destroy the building in Pátrai.

If Brognola jumped the gun on this, it could compromise Bolan's position and get him killed. If he waited, it might be too late when Bolan was ready for extraction. However, Brognola had to admit that the man had been in much worse positions before. The guy didn't need a baby-sitter, that was for sure, but he obviously didn't have the outside support of MI-6 as he'd thought he would.

"What do we know about Taylor's present location?" Brognola asked Price.

"We're not sure, but I'm working on that as my number-one priority. You're thinking of sending Jack to find her?"

"It had crossed my mind," Brognola said thoughtfully. "Maybe he could help her and find out where she really stands with MI-6."

"He also might be able to pinpoint the traitor working inside the British government," McCarter suggested helpfully.

Brognola nodded. "Okay, that's a start."

"What about this situation with the L3A, Hal?" Kurtzman said.

"Do you know where they're keeping the prototypes?"

"No, but I imagine we could find out."

"Do it and let me know as soon as possible. Maybe I can get the President involved in this and let him work the angle from his end. We're crossing into some pretty political arenas here, gang. We don't want to step on any toes."

"What about me, Hal?" McCarter chimed in. "You want me to go with Grimaldi?"

"Not this time, David," Brognola said. "With Katz in Israel, I think you're better suited to stay here with me and act as adviser on this one."

The Briton's face fell but he had apparently decided not to argue the point, which surprised Brognola. Normally he would have put up a fight for at least ten minutes, duking out the pros and cons with the Stony Man leader and then finally giving in as a matter of agreeing to disagree. And Brognola could see it in the Phoenix Force warrior's eyes, but McCarter didn't offer any further protest.

"That conference," Brognola continued, "is scheduled in less than seventy-two hours. If we can figure out where the prototypes are located before then, we might be able to get Jack inside to help Striker and buy additional time. I think 17 November feels it needs those weapons in order to make some sort of political statement."

"Do you think that if they aren't successful in getting the L3As," Price replied, "they'll forfeit the conference?"

"It's possible, but unlikely. Then they'll no longer have a need for Hyde-Baker, and they'll probably kill her. We have to allow Striker a chance to get her out. If his identity is compromised at that point, it won't matter. I think alerting the British about the L3As probably isn't a good idea."

"I don't know, Hal," McCarter said. "That's a lot of what-ifs. This could blow up in our faces."

"At least it gives us a chance to stall 17 November," Brognola pointed out.

"Fair enough," Kurtzman said.

"Okay, time's of the essence. Let's get cracking."

Even as the group broke up to set upon their individual tasks, Brognola wondered if there was really any point. With the meet between NATO and Greek officials only a couple of days away, and what little information they had to go on, the Stony Man leader knew their success would be based on chance and good fortune. But that was only the smallest part of it.

The rest fell on the shoulders of a man named Mack Bolan.

Athens, Greece

Dina Taylor sat waiting outside of Sir Radley Brygmart's office housed in the building at Constitution Square.

She didn't have to hear the conversation going on between Brygmart and the MI-6 foreign secretary for her to know that she was the subject of discussion. Nor did she have to know what the consequences could be for her decision. She'd probably sacrificed her career for Belasko, but she couldn't help herself. The guy was trying to do something good for both Britain and Greece.

What she couldn't understand was why Sir Brygmart didn't want to help the Americans. They were sent to aid in the rescue of the undersecretary, but it seemed to Taylor that recent MI-6 actions suggested anything but attaining that goal. Moreover, the Greek officials—like that lame-brained head of security in Pátrai—seemed to take a rather apathetic role in the apprehension of the 17 November gang.

Taylor's foresight in trying to warn Greek authorities about 17 November had afforded them an unheralded opportunity to arrest several key members in the group. Instead, they'd ignored her warnings and pleading until it no longer mattered. That incensed Taylor, and she thought that the Greek government could get what it deserved if it wasn't even willing to help its own people. The only problem was that the innocent citizens would go down with the sinking ship.

The door opened suddenly and Brygmart poked his head out. He didn't say anything to her. He just stared at her with those sad blue eyes a moment before gesturing that she should enter. Taylor stood, her legs quivering slightly as she entered his office and took a seat in front of the huge desk.

Brygmart pulled her out of the chair and hugged her fiercely. Taylor was surprised by his gruff gesture, but she quickly recovered as he broke the embrace and then gestured for her to sit. He didn't go around his desk but instead sat on the edge and folded his arms.

"I'm very disappointed in you, Dina," Brygmart said. "You disobeyed me. This is not only in direct violation of the articles governing conduct in the British secret service, but I consider it a personal affront."

"I'm sorry, Sir Brygmart, but—"

He raised his hand and cut in. "Please don't interrupt me and don't try to offer an argument. I'm not finished."

Taylor fell silent, a pain stabbing her heart as she thought about how she'd offended him. She could see the hurt in his eyes, and she knew he was probably going to have to discipline her rather severely. This wasn't a country club she worked for, and failure to obey orders was a very serious offense. Taylor didn't fear such reprisals as them sending her home and then hiring someone to kill her on the way. But she could be fired.

"At considerable length, the foreign secretary and I discussed your little stunts." He crossed around the desk now and began to gesture with his hand. "Both the unauthorized procurement of explosives, as well as your failure to report contact with the American agent. Not to mention your blatant disregard for the security of both yourself and this unit where that security official was concerned."

Brygmart shook his head as he sat behind the desk. "Under the circumstances, I've managed to convey to the foreign secretary that you are a young, passionate agent with an impeccable record. I had to remind him that these were the gravest of circumstances, considering the life of Undersecretary Hyde-Baker is at risk. He concurred with my assessment. Fortunately, after some very quick talking on my part, I've convinced him not to discharge you from the service."

Taylor let out a sigh of relief.

She was lucky and she knew it. Such violations could have resulted in much worse consequences. At best, she knew a reassignment was coming but she could somehow bear that. It didn't carry with it nearly the shame it would have if she'd been kicked out. Not even the SAS would have taken her back. She would have been lucky to find a job as a hostess in some lodging house in the country.

"The foreign secretary also agreed that you were a bit impetuous, and that a more experienced and knowledgeable field agent was appropriate for this assignment," Brygmart continued in a consternate tone. He looked at her and sighed. "Therefore, you will leave here and return to your quarters under escort. I would suggest that you pack your personal belongings and report for duty at the London office in one week. You are remanded to clerical duties until further notice."

"What?" Taylor rebutted, suddenly angered by the punishment. "But you said I had an excellent record. Why would they pull me from the field?"

"You are fortunate they have not pulled you from active duty," Brygmart reminded her gruffly. "Do you think that I like this, Dina? Do you think that I'm happy that this has happened? You have no idea how it pains me to do this."

"Yes, sir," Taylor replied quietly. "Sir Brygmart?"

"Yes?"

"I'm sorry I did not follow orders. I would never have done anything against you personally. You know that."

"Of course I do," Brygmart replied gently. "But I've also learned that if you are to be successful in this kind of game, you must learn how to obey your superior officers. You could have seriously compromised our position here. It's only my connections within the Greek government that will keep things quiet about our involvement with the Pátrai incident."

Taylor had no answer for him because she knew he was right. Not only had she revealed her role as an MI-6 agent operating in the country, but she'd also nearly blown Mike Belasko's cover. It was a good bet that her face or name might come back to Midas, and that would most definitely blow the deal. She'd been damn stupid and all because of a Yank agent with high ideals.

"And the officer who supplied you this inventory?" he continued, tapping a folder on his desk. "He's been discharged and arrested for criminal subversion. You could have ended in the same straits had I not protected you."

"What about Belasko?" she asked. "They may find out he tried to set a trap for them. Or possibly that he blew them in Pátrai. What are you going to do for him?"

"I'm sorry, Dina," Brygmart said in a low, even voice, "but you cannot ask me to risk this agency for the life of one American. He knew the risks, just like you, and he chose to take them."

"You speak of him as if he were dead, sir." Taylor couldn't conceal the bitter edge in her voice.

"If they discovered he caused their failure, as you say," he retorted, "he is dead. And even if they haven't, there is no possible way that he can maintain this masquerade for long. They will eventually figure out he's a traitor and kill him."

"I don't believe that," Taylor argued. "I don't think it would be quite that easy. This man is different...somehow. I don't know, but I just think we should give him the benefit of the doubt."

"You're allowing this foolish American to cloud your judgment," Brygmart replied with a dismissive wave. "I can see that the sooner I get you back to London the better off we'll be. You leave tomorrow afternoon on a diplomatic flight. I'm afraid I'll have to keep you under armed escort until you are back in London."

He stood and reached out his hand. "I must ask you to surrender your weapon."

Taylor stared at him a moment, trying to keep her hands from trembling. Finally she stood and reached beneath the blazer she was wearing. She retrieved the Walther PPK, unloaded the weapon and placed both parts in Brygmart's open palm. He took them gently and placed them in his desk drawer.

THE TUNNELS of 17 November's underground base seemed more encompassing and foreboding than Mack Bolan had remembered them.

The Executioner knew part of it was the feeling of dread he couldn't seem to shake. The numbers were ticking down, and Bolan knew he wasn't even close to devising a plan that could shut the group down once and for all. Right at the moment, Bolan would have given anything to pull himself out and come back with guns blazing.

But he knew it wouldn't do him a bit of good. Bolan had only worked with part of the group. They didn't tend to cluster themselves together and so he knew that destroying them would require action in piecemeal. A few here and a few there—much like he'd done in eliminating Guilio and Endre. That was the only way he could take out 17 November.

Eradication of their organization in full was paramount to success. Sure, others would probably rise in the future to terrorize Greece, probably even calling themselves by the same name. But Bolan dealt with the present—he couldn't do a thing about the future because that belonged to the citizens. When they were ready to elect leaders that weren't afraid to take a stand against the evils of society, that's when real change could begin.

Such efforts had proved successful time and again throughout history. From the moment the first shot was fired in the American Revolution to the response of the Allied powers against Adolf Hitler, people had repeatedly demonstrated their ability to suppress tyranny when doing so under a united front.

The war against terrorism was no different. War Everlasting was a self-explanatory concept. It didn't matter if it was against powers or principalities, terrorists or common thugs, drug dealers or sadistic governments. The net result was strength in numbers. Terrorists would never succeed against a country united in its views, and one that had policies in place to deal harshly with such crimes and respond to violence with violence. Sometimes it was the only way when attempts at a peaceful resolution failed.

At least it was a way that worked for the Executioner.

"I have arranged for you to speak with the British politician," Helonas said, entering the living area where Bolan had set up some makeshift quarters. "She awaits you in a special anteroom I've set up."

"I want to talk to her alone," Bolan said.

"I cannot allow that, Michalis," Helonas replied quickly. "You haven't earned that kind of trust yet."

Bolan shook his head. "I like to work alone in situations like this. More than one person makes these techniques less effective. I promise I won't hurt her too badly. At least not in such a way that she won't recover."

Helonas thought seriously about Bolan's request, and then finally shook his head. "No, I'm sorry. Until we find out who betrayed us, the group has decided nobody works freelance."

"Fine."

The soldier rose and followed Helonas down one of the long corridors. Their footsteps echoed within the confines of the narrow walkway. The ever present smell of raw sewage permeated everything, and Bolan wondered when he'd have the opportunity to bathe. He'd gone two days without a shower now and he was beginning to detect his own body odor.

He decided to mention it to Helonas.

"Perhaps after you have finished, I can take you aboveground and we'll visit a shower area. There are several decent ones nearby."

"Or maybe I could just go to my sister's place." He reached into his pocket and showed Helonas a key. "I've got free access any time I need it."

Helonas nodded with a smile. "Perhaps. I would like to meet your sister anyway. Midas tells me she is quite beautiful."

"I wouldn't know," Bolan said. "I've never really thought about it."

"Ah, here we are." Helonas pushed through a heavy metal door that had been fashioned to fit a hole in the wall. A smaller tunnel branched off the main one, and Bolan could barely discern a woman tied to a chair in the dim lights. She had silvery hair and a prominent chin protruding from a bruised, swollen jaw. Her eyes were concealed behind a blindfold, but Bolan knew she wouldn't recognize him anyway.

Helonas ripped off the blindfold. "Good morning. I would like you to meet a friend of mine. His name is Michalis, and he wants to ask you some questions."

"What does he really want, Mr. Helonas?" Hyde-Baker said, not looking at the man and lowering her eyes some. "Does he want to beat me, as well?"

Bolan could barely understand what she was saying. Her tongue was swollen from lack of water and she smelled of urine and feces. They hadn't even let her relieve herself properly. One thing was certain: a woman that age didn't have the physical constitution to endure much more of this kind of treatment.

Bolan had to find a way to get her out of there and quick.

The Executioner put on his best interrogation face and said, "Cyril tells me you don't want to cooperate." A knife blade rasped from its sheath, and Bolan drew his thumb across it gently. "I'm sorry to hear that."

"What are you going to do with me?" Hyde-Baker asked, trembling visibly.

"Nothing, if you want to start talking," Bolan answered quietly.

The soldier wondered how he was going to make good on the threat if the British diplomat remained obstinate and resisted questioning. After all, she didn't know that her saving grace now stood before her. Mack Bolan was the only thing standing between Hyde-Baker and whatever horrible death 17 November had devised for her. Once they had the information on the L3A, the woman was probably as good as dead.

Bolan stepped forward and knelt next to her. He clamped his hand down on one of her hands and reached two fingers around her thumb. He put the tip of the knife against the underside edge of her nails and flashed her a frosty smile.

"I've been in places," he said, "where people had to confess their crimes before they could seek absolution. It didn't matter if they were guilty or not. Tell us where they're hiding these weapons, and we can bypass all this unnecessary displeasure."

"I will tell you nothing," Hyde-Baker said vehemently. "You can kill me if you like."

"You will not get off that easy, Madam Secretary," Helonas cut in.

The door opened suddenly with a scrape of metal on rock. A dark-haired man stood there and his eyes flicked toward Bolan. The Executioner gave the newcomer a level stare, and it took him a moment to recognize him. It was the man in the picture Barbara Price had shown him. The one who had arranged the meet with Taylor.

The man looked at Helonas and something desperate filled his features.

"Midas, what are you doing here?" Helonas scolded. "You know you're never to come here like this."

"I must speak to you," he whispered in Greek. The Executioner could understand that much, although the guy thought he was being clever. "Alone."

"We're busy," Helonas countered in English.

Midas said something else, and Helonas threw up his hands with disgust. He turned to the Executioner and said, "You must forgive my cousin. He is young and insolent at best. Wait here and I will be right back."

Fate was smiling on Bolan. With these two out of the room, the Executioner had his chance alone with Hyde-Baker. The thought probably hadn't even occurred to Helonas, and he wasn't about to mention it. If he could get even one minute alone with her, it would be enough to assure Hyde-Baker. If the British politician had hope, she could survive long enough to facilitate a rescue.

The two men left the room and closed the door behind them.

Bolan looked at Hyde-Baker and flashed her a reassuring smile. "Madam Secretary? We don't have a lot of time, so I need you to listen to me very carefully. I'm not here to hurt you—I'm here to help you."

"What?" she muttered thickly. "What are you saying? Who are you?"

"Just listen. My name is Belasko. Seventeen November's primary purpose is to stop the conference, and they plan to use the L3As to do it."

"What are you here for?" she asked blankly.

"To stop them. Permanently." He shook his head, wishing she would be quiet so he could give his information. "And to get you out. But I need you tell me where these weapons are. It will buy me some time, not to mention it will keep you alive long enough for me to formulate a plan."

"How do I know this isn't some trick?"

"Do you know the name Dina Taylor?"

"I don't think so," she said suspiciously.

Damn. Bolan had hoped she would know Taylor and that would be enough to prove he was telling the truth. He thought fast. "Look, I know that Kermit Albertson is scheduled to testify at the conference. Now, would a member of 17 November have that information?"

She snorted and then coughed. Bloody flecks dotted her shirt as she hacked. "Okay, so what if I decide to believe you? A second ago you were ready to stick a knife under my fingernails."

"No, I wasn't," he said. "Look, Madam Secretary, we don't have time to argue about this. I've already killed two of these terrorists. The group is doomed, but I can't do it by myself. You have to trust me."

"I guess," she said after looking in those hard blue eyes, "that I have nothing to lose."

"That's true."

"Okay, I'll tell you."

"I'm listening."

"The prototypes are being held at the Wellsboro Company printing factory in Portsmouth. The storage crates were delivered months ago, listed as machine parts for United Kingdom Press."

Bolan nodded. "I'll find it."

The door opened suddenly, and Helonas gestured for Bolan to come out.

The Executioner nodded, rose and scowled at Hyde-Baker and then walked out. Helonas closed the door and didn't speak to Bolan. He followed Helonas down the corridor and back in the direction of the quarters area.

Midas accompanied them, not saying a word to the Executioner, either. Something was definitely up, and Bolan prepared himself for a possible shoot-out there and then. Nonetheless, there was a part of their behavior that had Bolan curious about what news Midas had brought.

Helonas continued past the quarters and led them to the briefing room where they'd planned the bombing of the political building. He gestured at a seat and then pulled one up himself. The two sat facing each other while Midas stood behind Helonas. The two men stared at Bolan hard for a long time. The Executioner waited, meeting the challenge with an icy stare of his own.

"What's going on?" he finally asked.

"What's going on," Helonas echoed, "is that Midas says we have a traitor in our midst."

"I've been saying that for a while now, Cyril," Bolan replied quickly. "Somebody blew us at Pátrai. There's no question in my mind. Those security people—"

"The rest of the group thinks it is you," Midas interrupted.

The soldier threw a warning look at Midas and said, "Who are you anyway, pal? If we've got a problem here, then I say let the group decide about me in a vote. Don't just come in here shooting off your mouth."

"Let's not become defensive," Helonas said. He gave Midas a nasty look of his own and continued, "We are all brothers

Accepting your 2 free books and gift places you under no obligation to buy anything. You may keep the books and gift and return the shipping statement marked "cancel." If you do not cancel, about a month later we'll send you 6 additional novels and bill you just $26.70* — that's a saving of 15% off the cover price of all 6 books! And there's no extra charge for shipping! You may cancel at any time, but if you choose to continue, every other month we'll send you 6 more books, which you may either purchase at the discount price or return to us and cancel your subscription.

*Terms and prices subject to change without notice. Sales tax applicable in N.Y. Canadian residents will be charged applicable provincial taxes and GST.

here. This is my cousin, who I told you about. The nephew of my father and our connection in the Greek cabinet."

Bolan fell silent a moment, then lowered his head, shaking it with a broad grin. He looked back at Helonas and said, "What do you think about me, Cyril? Do you think I'm a traitor?"

"I don't know what to think, Michalis." The tone in his voice was genuine as he added, "I would like to think it is not you."

"Well, maybe you'll think differently when I tell you that I know where the L3As are."

"What?" There was a look of total disbelief on his face. "How did you find out?"

Bolan jerked his thumb in the direction of Hyde-Baker's makeshift prison.

"Do you know how long—?" Helonas began, but he changed his mind. "Forget it. Such matters are unimportant. Where are these weapons?"

"In Portsmouth," the Executioner replied. "But I would suggest we don't tell anyone until we've planned the operation, picked the team and made it to England."

"Agreed. I will leave the planning to you. It will be a chance to redeem yourself, my friend."

Yeah, the Executioner would plan the operation all right. He'd continue to manipulate the situation until all the pieces were in place. And when the time was right, Mack Bolan would eradicate 17 November and put an end to the terrorists' reign of terror. When the moment came, he'd turn the tables on them with such speed and fury it was unlikely they would ever recover.

And timing would be everything.

AS BOLAN AND Helonas parked in front of Taylor's house, the Executioner immediately sensed something was out of place.

There was a nondescript sedan parked in the driveway—definitely not hers—and the house seemed oddly quiet. Bolan had learned to trust his intuition over the years, and this night it was telling him there was trouble ahead. He turned to look at

Helonas in the passenger seat, and the terrorist read his expression.

"What's wrong?" he asked.

The Executioner didn't want to arouse Helonas's suspicions so he shrugged. "She's got company."

"What kind of company?"

"I don't know," Bolan growled, "but I don't like it."

"Well," said Helonas, getting out of the car, "let's go see who she's entertaining."

Bolan saw an unavoidable confrontation and jumped out to intercept the Greek terrorist. He stepped in Helonas's way and flashed him a wan smile. "Maybe we'd better do this a little more carefully."

Helonas clapped him on the shoulder. "You're acting as if you have something to hide, Michalis."

"I've got nothing to hide. I just don't know what's going on in there." He jerked his thumb over his shoulder at the sedan and added, "That's not her car."

That caused Helonas to raise his eyebrows. "Do you think there might be trouble?"

"Maybe, maybe not," Bolan countered, "but I'd hate to find out the hard way."

"Okay," Helonas finally said with a sigh, looking past Bolan at the house again. "She is your sister, my friend. How do you want to do this?"

"I'll take the front, you go to the back. She usually keeps that door open. Give me five minutes and then get inside. But let's do it quietly. I don't want to alert anyone if there is trouble waiting."

Helonas nodded and stepped around the soldier, sticking to the hedgerow on the far side of the driveway as he made for the back.

As Bolan walked casually toward the front door, he could detect a fresh set of noises. And whatever was going on inside, it didn't sound friendly. The Executioner could hear one man yelling and the lights in the front window suddenly flickered.

Bolan sensed the trouble as he sprinted for the front door, snagging his Beretta from shoulder leather on the run.

He put his foot to the front door and it crashed inward, splintering on the hinges.

Bolan followed through with the Desert Eagle .44 clutched in his fist and looked for a target.

As Dina Taylor stared at the body of her escort, who now lay in the middle of the floor, she wondered what she'd bloody well gotten herself into.

The man who stood before her was tall and swarthy, with closely cropped brown hair, and muscles that bulged through his shirt and slacks. He looked a lot like Belasko, but there was something sinister behind the brown eyes. He was dark and heartless—she could tell because she'd met men like him before.

His colleagues called him Zeus, although she doubted that was anything more than a cover name. Yes, there was something definitely hard about her new captor, and Taylor surmised it was going to be long night. A very long night if the two large cords with brass ends that sparked and dimmed the lights were any indication.

The British MI-6 agent cursed herself for letting these cretins take her and Carney by surprise. Poor Dale Carney, a brand-new father whose daughter would now have to grow up without him. Taylor had met Carney's wife, Nephra, on one or two occasions. She was a beautiful Egyptian woman Carney had met on assignment—the two were soon married after meeting, and little Shanaraya was born less than a year later.

Taylor would make sure they paid for taking away the little girl's father if she got free.

Taylor's wrists were raw where she'd try to work loose from the heavy ropes that bound her to the cherry-wood settee. The men had knocked her unconscious and waited until she was awake before shooting Carney in the head.

Then they rigged up this crude electric-shock system to the fuse box and stripped her to her panties. Several buckets full of cold water later, Taylor sat on the couch and shivered. These bastards had humiliated her, killed a good man and now they were going to ask her questions that if not answered properly would likely meet with 100 amps of misery.

There were five other men in the room besides the leader, and all were toting a variety of hardware. A couple held machine pistols beneath their arms that dangled on straps over their shoulders. Still others had the bulges of pistols beneath their coats. They were a well-armed group of various ethnic backgrounds, and that left Taylor to only guess who they might be or whom they worked for.

She gritted her teeth as one of the new arrivals came nearer with the terminals. He cracked them together while the man called Zeus watched behind him with satisfaction.

"What the hell do you want to know?" Taylor asked him. "You haven't even asked me any questions."

"I don't want to know anything, my dear," Zeus replied.

"Then what do you want from me?"

"I want your soul from you," he whispered with hatred in his voice. "I want to take the very breath from you."

"Go to hell," Taylor managed.

She braced herself as Zeus nodded toward his minion. The man with the terminals was practically drooling as he stepped forward and prepared to deliver the first shock to her.

Taylor watched as he drew closer and closer. She was trained to resist all forms of torture, but she knew the reality here was much different. It was frustrating to think that they weren't doing this to extract information, but simply because they found some perverse pleasure in electrocuting her to death. It took a sick mind to conjure that, and she hoped that if Belasko ever completed his mission that he'd hunt these dogs down and kill them in their sleep.

She clenched her teeth as the first terminal was placed against her abdomen.

Shouts of surprise immediately followed the crashing sound of a door giving in under tremendous pressure. All faces turned in time to see a specter of death come through the front door, clad in dark clothes and black leather jacket.

And there was no mistaking the cannon in his fist.

MACK BOLAN RENDERED his first judgment on a short, thin man who was reaching inside his jacket for his pistol.

The 230-grain .44 slug bored through the man's skull and shattered cranial bones on its way out the back. The man behind him was sprayed by his comrade's blood even as he reached for his Uzi subgun.

Bolan fired a second round, the weapon discharging a thunderous report as his second target met the same fate. The round ripped away the lower jaw and part of the neck, spinning the man in a pirouette before slamming him to the ground. Sheer pandemonium took up the rest of the fray as the remaining combatants went for cover.

One man dived behind an overstuffed rocker and leveled his pistol across the back. Bolan easily slid behind the cover of the wall as his opponent popped off several shots. The rounds either slammed into the wall or sailed well past the intended target.

The Executioner crouched, swinging his pistol around the corner and getting sight acquisition by aiming at a point midway down the back of the chair. Bolan fired three shots in succession, and blood spewed from the man's mouth moments after large holes appeared in the overlay material. The heavy caliber rounds had made short work of the chair, continuing on a straight course through the back and into the man's chest. The gunman slid from view behind the chair.

Bolan popped the clip and reloaded a second as Helonas appeared in the doorway at the end of the hall. The Walther P-38 was clutched in his hand and he pressed his back against the wall. Bolan nodded briefly to him and then finished loading the weapon, letting the slide come forward with a resounding clang.

Helonas came around the corner of the hall where it entered the living room through a second foyer and sighted on something unseen. He squeezed the trigger twice, and Bolan knew that one of their enemies had to be on the opposing end. It seemed ironic that the Greek terrorist who he would ultimately bring down in much the same fashion was now helping him to do the same to his own enemies.

Bolan came around the corner and found his next target trying to grab better cover. These men obviously hadn't expected the Executioner to show when he did, not to mention Helonas. This hadn't played out the way they planned, and Bolan meant to keep them off balance while he could make it good.

The gunman scurrying to find better cover saw the wraith-like form tracking on him and tried to bring his SMG to bear. The Desert Eagle jumped twice in Bolan's viselike grip as he rapidly sighted on the target center mass. The bullets punched through the gunner's upper torso, flipping him off his feet and crashing him through a china cabinet. His body landed on the carpet amidst a hail of blood and broken glass.

A cold, hard silence fell on the place. Bolan and Helonas stood frozen, pistols up and tracking the room, waiting for any further resistance. Only after a half a minute had elapsed did the Executioner finally relax. He holstered his weapon and told Helonas to check the rest of the house while he rushed to help Taylor.

He used a pocket knife to cut the ropes and then sat her up gently.

"I'm okay, Michalis," she managed with a weak smile.

He nodded, went to a nearby bedroom and returned with a towel and a quilt. He handed her the towel so she could dry her hair and quickly wrapped the quilt around her exposed flesh. She shivered inside the blanket as she rubbed her hair vigorously. She looked like a mess with her body soaked and her blond locks standing on end, but aside from that she appeared unharmed.

"You got here just in time," she told the Executioner in a whisper.

"Looks like," he replied quietly with a smile. "Listen, I don't have time to explain but I'm leaving tomorrow morning for Portsmouth. I've also located Hyde-Baker. When I'm ready, I'm going to bring down the whole show at once."

She nodded and said quickly, "What's in Portsmouth?"

Bolan shook her off as Helonas returned to where they sat and tossed them a quick nod. "It's all clear. I disconnected those cables, too."

"Thanks," Bolan said. "I owe you."

Helonas nodded and then looked at Taylor. "Are you okay, my dear?"

"Yes, I'm fine."

"Cyril, I'd like you to meet my sister, Diona Crysanthos. Diona, this is Cyril Helonas."

Taylor poked an arm out from the quilt to shake his hand but instead he bent over and kissed it. The Executioner could see the revulsion screw up her features when Helonas wasn't looking, but he remained silent.

"Pleasure," Taylor said.

"Oh, no," Helonas replied, gently releasing her hand. "The pleasure is all mine. Your brother speaks very highly of you."

Taylor turned to look at Bolan. "I'll bet."

"He also tells me you are the one who got the explosives for us," Helonas continued. "You have the thanks of some very important people."

"They wouldn't happen to be the same people who just tried to kill me, would they?" she asked haughtily. "Because if they are, I don't bloody well like it."

"You recognize any of these guys, Cyril?" Bolan asked.

"No," he said, shaking his head.

He turned his attention to Taylor and added, "I have no idea who these people are, my dear, but I can assure you they do not work with our organization. They are much too savage."

"You have no idea why they wanted to kill you," Bolan continued.

"No," she replied, "I didn't recognize any of them. Although it looks like their leader managed to slip away. They called him Zeus."

Bolan looked questioningly at Helonas, who just shook his head and shrugged.

The Executioner nodded and then gestured to Carney. "Who was that?"

"My date," she said.

"I'm sorry," he replied.

"I am, too. I just met him. What are you going to do now?"

"I have something I need to take care of," he replied. "Are you going to be okay?"

"Yes, I'm leaving for England first thing tomorrow morning. Frankly, I can't wait to get back and see London again. I have some very important artwork I'm going to get at auction there."

"Well," Bolan said, rising from the couch, "stay in touch."

"Michalis," Helonas interjected, "are you just going to leave her alone?"

"Why not?" he said. "She's a tough nut and she can take care of herself. Whoever pulled this job isn't coming back. Besides, you heard her say she's leaving tomorrow morning."

"Not very chivalrous of you, my friend," Helonas said.

He looked at Taylor. "And what about the police? I imagine they will arrive soon."

"I sincerely doubt it," Taylor said sarcastically "Most of the people who live in the other houses have left for the winter. This whole block is practically deserted. If they do show up, knocking on my door, I will think of something to tell them."

"Yeah, and if the police are going to show up," Bolan reminded him, "we need to get out here now."

"I suppose you are correct. We do have other, more pressing matters that require our attention."

"Right, so let's go."

Helonas nodded and then turned to leave.

Taylor threw Bolan a pleading look, but he knew there was nothing he could do about it. It was unlikely Helonas would give them a few minutes alone, although whoever it was that had attacked Taylor reinforced the idea in Helonas's mind that Bolan was on his side. Certainly the Executioner wouldn't set up his own sister for a hit, so that meant there was somebody else at the center of all this mess.

And Mack Bolan added the name Zeus to his list of enemies.

LENNOX BARONE—aka Zeus—was angry.

He was angry at the incompetence of his men, and he was angry at the fact he'd lost five in this last escapade. He was angry with the Greeks and the British, and he was angry with Nemo Amphionides for handing him this putrid assignment. He was also angry that these ambitious simpletons couldn't manage their own affairs, let alone those of an entire government or nation.

But most of all he was angry with himself.

He'd known of the American's reputation, but he underestimated him anyway. Nothing could get him killed faster than doing such a thing. Belasko worked for the American government, in some capacity. Barone's contacts were well acquainted with everyone, and they informed him that Belasko didn't actually belong to 17 November. In fact, he was there to destroy the renegade group.

As Barone rode in a cab bound for the downtown area of Athens, he began to wonder if there weren't a simpler way to destroy the American and the British pig. She was under orders to return to London immediately, according to his sources.

Perhaps there was another way to eliminate the two. Yes, Barone could already see how this would fit perfectly into his plans. He could destroy them without firing a shot, and that thought made his trip more comfortable. He would simply recruit some of Amphionides's men to do the dirty work. After he'd finished his business here, he would contact the deputy justice minister and demand a new deal.

The cabbie deposited him in a quiet, traditional neighborhood street. The houses were crammed together, and that would make Barone's job so much easier. He walked through the neighborhood several times.

After doing a thorough recon, the assassin returned to his original starting point and located the home of his target. He squeezed between it and a neighboring house, and looked up into a window. The target sat in an adjoining room with his back to the window, spooning soup from a bowl as he read some official-looking documents.

What a fool! The fact that this doddering, old man held rank in one of the largest and most respected espionage organizations in the world seemed like a laughable concept to Barone. He'd worked for quite a few of the major agencies throughout the years as a freelancer, taking the jobs where they could maintain plausible deniability, and if he'd learned anything it was that people like Brygmart didn't want to dirty their hands.

That well-manicured British snobbery might have had a place in the political arena, but there was no room for it in this game. Assassination was business as usual in the business of government versus government. Intelligence was the number-one product, and it was served on a plate full of skullduggery and treachery.

How many people throughout history had died in the name of "national security"? Important people disappeared into thin air and within a couple of months nobody gave it another thought. Planes blew up and politicians with powerful ties just dropped out of sight or mysteriously ended up dead from some fatal disease they didn't know they had until it was too late.

The truth was evident if one really wanted to acknowledge it.

Barone had learned to accept it, and that made his profession both satisfying and rewarding. While money was certainly a factor, it didn't bring nearly as much satisfaction as watching powers rise and fall again and again, their having never learned that what was sowed would eventually be reaped.

Pride cometh before the fall, Barone thought.

He eased the window open and crawled through the frame,

watching quietly for any sign that the Briton detected him. Some kind of raucous music was playing on a radio and it seemed to mask the small noises Barone made as he entered the house.

Once inside, the assassin closed the window and crept up behind the man. He reached into his coat and withdrew the Taurus 76 .32-caliber long pistol with a sound suppressor. The weapon was primarily a target revolver, but its medium frame made it a bit more practical for such uses as this one.

Barone pointed the barrel at the back of the man's head and squeezed the trigger twice. Both of the rimfire .32 S&W long slugs drilled into his skull, driving bone fragments into the brain and effectively ending the British agent's life. Sir Radley Brygmart's head fell forward into his soup, and blood began to trickle down his nape.

Barone silently holstered his pistol and then looked quickly at the documents. They didn't appear to contain any information of importance, just some kind of standard paperwork. Zeus took the folder anyway and slipped it inside his overcoat. He then looked around the room before walking around and turning off all of the lights.

He finally returned to the dining room, looked at Brygmart one more time without emotion and then went to the front door. He killed the hallway light and porch light before leaving the house. The neighborhood was quiet outside, and Barone inhaled a breath of fresh air before walking down the street in the direction of Constitution Square.

He'd accomplished one-third of his job. And very shortly, he would see to the elimination of Belasko and the British bitch.

And then his mission would be complete.

THE PHONE JANGLED on the bedside table and startled Nemo Amphionides from his sleep. The deputy justice minister gazed at the old pocket watch on his table before reaching over and picking up the receiver. Whoever was calling him at this hour was going to pay for it if this wasn't important.

"Yes?" he mumbled.

"It's me," the cultured voice with the European accent replied.

Amphionides turned over in bed to look at his wife, listening a moment to her steady breathing. She had become accustomed to the phone calls at weird hours since his appointment as DJM, and this time the ringing hadn't awakened her. There was some deity to thank for small favors.

"Why are you calling me here?" Amphionides asked. "If this were traced—"

"It cannot be traced," Zeus replied, "so you may forgo the melodrama. I called to let you know that one-half of your problem has been solved."

"Which half?"

"The older half."

Amphionides understood the reference, nodding as a smile played across his lips. It was just as well. With Brygmart out of the way, he knew he could rest easier. But if only one-half of the problem was solved, that meant the Taylor woman lived.

"What about the other half?"

"I ran into some trouble with the American. It is as you had told me. This man is resourceful and dangerous. A most formidable opponent. I should not have underestimated him."

"Underestimated in what way?"

"That is unimportant. What is important is that I'm afraid my price must change. If you want this man eliminated as well, it will cost you extra."

"We had a deal," Amphionides said, looking back at his wife, who stirred in the bed. He whispered tightly, "You told me he would be at no extra cost."

"That was before I knew who he was."

"What do you mean?"

"This man is working for the Americans—that much I'm sure of. I don't know his name or the organizations for which he operates, but I can tell you that he is a professional combatant. He could prove quite dangerous...to both of us. I lost five good men to him. It is only reasonable I should seek compensation for my losses."

"All right," Amphionides conceded, "I'm not going to argue about this. How much extra?"

"You take me too literally. I don't seek monetary compensation but rather...replacements. Give me three of your best men from that personal team you have. And don't bother to deny it because I know about your little operation against the train."

Amphionides thought about it a moment and decided not to attempt a lie. "You want me to pay you, plus give you three of my own men? That goes outside our deal."

"That is business, I'm afraid," Zeus replied evenly. "Unless you would just like me to finish with the Englishwoman and forget about this American. He could then be your problem."

"Just see to it that it's done. I'll send the men immediately, but you don't get the rest of your fee until you can show me proof positive that the British agent is taken care of. Understood?"

"Yes, understood."

"Now, my contact tells me the American and his group are planning to steal something in Portsmouth. I'm going to alert the British authorities of this, and see to it that they are aware of the situation. This way the British can clean up the mess on their own territory, and this leaves us in the clear. Nonetheless, you must still go to London and eliminate the woman."

"Consider it done," Zeus replied, and he broke the connection.

This new piece of information troubled Amphionides as he hung up the phone. He probably wasn't going to be able to go back to sleep. He lay in the comfort of his bed and wondered just how much trouble he'd taken upon himself. The meeting was in less than two days. By that time, 17 November was scheduled to be in position to eradicate these egotists from NATO and other governments.

And then, of course, there was the execution of this witness they claimed to have. To date, nobody in Amphionides circle could identify this individual, but that wouldn't be the case forever. Eventually he would discover who it was and have him killed, as well. Then he would rush into the fray as the savior to the adoration of his new constituents.

Interference in the Greek way of life was about to come to an end. And it would only be a matter of time before he could then insert himself into the office of prime minister by eradicating Cyril's friends once and for all. He would be hailed as a national hero and his political career would be secured.

It was only a matter of time.

Jack Grimaldi turned the Gulfstream C-21A jet over the Peloponnisos on his final approach into Olympic Airport. He dipped the nose as he skimmed above Syngrou, a major avenue that ran down the center of Athens.

The Aegean Sea was spread out on one side, and Mount Hymettus filled the cockpit view on the other through the early-morning mists. Dawn was breaking over the horizon and although he was exhausted, Grimaldi could barely contain his excitement. It had been a long time since his last trip to Greece. That one had been pleasure, however.

This time it was different—much different. He had very little time remaining to locate Dina Taylor and, in turn, the Executioner.

Trouble was brewing on the horizon; the Stony Man ace pilot could feel it in his gut, although he knew there was very little he could do about it. It sounded like Bolan really had his hands full this time. Seventeen November was a radical and dangerous group, and if Bolan's cover was blown he was probably going to need a lift out of there and quick. Jack Grimaldi intended to be the wings of that eagle.

The Stony Man pilot's credentials got him immediate landing clearance and through customs without a hassle. He soon had his rental car and set off for Taylor's place, which intelligence said was in an uptown area of the city. His instructions were actually simple: find Taylor and Bolan, and then assist the soldier in whatever plans he might have formulated.

That was something the crack flier could do. He'd seen the big guy through too many scrapes to count, and this one wasn't going to be any different. Grimaldi no longer felt he owed the Executioner a debt of redemption. He'd easily paid it back over the years, and then some. Besides the fact there was no such thing as an unpaid debt among friends. Bolan was fighting for the little guy, and Grimaldi wanted to be on the right team for the big win. The team was headed by Mack Bolan, and that's all the convincing Grimaldi needed.

The Stony Man pilot arrived at Taylor's house and studied the exterior. It was a nice place, set in the upscale suburban sprawl of Athens. If there was such a thing as upscale here. While Athens was beautiful with gorgeous historical landmarks, it was dirty. Environmental protection and sanitation weren't exactly strong suits where the local government was concerned.

Grimaldi pulled his car into the drive and went to the front door. He rang the bell and a moment later he was greeted by a long-legged blonde with flashy eyes and a body to die for. Based on McCarter's description, there was little doubt in Grimaldi's mind he was looking at Dina Taylor.

"Can I help you?" she asked. Her lovely chest heaved as she panted.

"Uh, I don't know. Am I interrupting anything?" Grimaldi asked.

"I'm just trying to pack," she said. She arched an eyebrow and tossed a fist on her hip. "But if I had to venture a guess, I'd say you're one of those Yanks working with Belasko. Right?"

Grimaldi tossed her a cocksure grin. "That would be me."

She inclined her head as she stepped aside. "Come on in."

Taylor closed the door and walked past him into a nearby bedroom. Grimaldi noticed the bodies, broken glass and congealed blood strewed about an adjoining living room.

The pilot followed Taylor into the bedroom and immediately noticed a suitcase was spread out on the bed, recklessly stuffed with a hodge-podge of clothes and undergarments. It appeared the MI-6 agent was leaving in a big hurry, and that made Grimaldi nervous.

"What's the rush?" he asked.

"I've got a plane to catch," she said, yanking some more clothes from the closet hangers and tossing them haphazardly into the suitcase.

"Okay. So I ask again, what's the rush?"

She stopped and looked harshly at him. "Listen, um—"

"The name's Jack."

"Okay, Jack, listen up. Mike Belasko's gotten himself into some serious trouble."

Grimaldi could immediately feel his heartbeat increase. He knew it! The Executioner was in some kind of a scrape and now blondie here was about to beat feet on him. Well, Grimaldi had accomplished half of his mission and he wasn't about to screw it up now.

"What kind of trouble?"

"The kind I can't fix from here. He was here last night," she added with a wave toward the living room, "in case you didn't notice."

Grimaldi jerked his thumb over his shoulder. "He did that?"

She nodded. "Him and one of the higher-ups within 17 November that he's befriended."

"Well," Grimaldi retorted, folding his arms, "would you like to stop packing long enough to tell me what the hell is going on?"

"I'd like to but I can't. I have to get to England before they do."

"Who is 'they'?"

"Seventeen November. They have some kind of operation planned in Portsmouth, but I didn't have time to find out what it was. I don't even know where this operation is going down. That's why I have to get to the home office in London and find out."

Grimaldi nodded. "My people surmised that 17 November might try to steal the L3A."

Taylor stopped packing and looked at him. She was a beautiful woman, no doubt about it, but she was also a hardened professional spy. Grimaldi wasn't sure he could really trust anything she was saying at this point. Despite McCarter's reservations, the ace flier wasn't completely convinced Taylor hadn't gone dirty. Nonetheless, she wouldn't have stood here telling him all of this stuff if she didn't want to. She could have just shot him dead when he wasn't looking.

And while that wasn't much to go on, it was a step in the right direction.

"The new antiterrorist weapon?" Taylor asked. "But how would they know to look in Portsmouth?"

"I don't know," Grimaldi said, "but someone might have already alerted your government. If they're planning to steal the L3A, they won't get away with it."

"What!" Taylor exclaimed, asked him incredulously. "No! We've got to stop them. We've got to call it off!"

"What are you talking about?" Grimaldi demanded.

"Belasko took a great risk to get this information to me. He even put his own cover in jeopardy. He's located the undersecretary and developed a plan to take them all down at the same time. Any interference by my government now could prove detrimental to those plans!"

"Oh, great," Grimaldi moaned. "We thought that Belasko was in trouble, maybe even dead. Somebody apparently told my people that you had disappeared, abandoned him or something, and that they thought he might be dead."

"That's ridiculous!" Taylor snapped. "I'm the only one who has been helping him. The rest of my people seem to want to write him off at every chance they get."

This was definitely not good. If he believed what Taylor was telling him, and he had no reason to doubt her at that point, the British would be waiting for the group. That could mean significant bloodshed, and it could also prove disastrous if Bolan got caught in the cross fire. He had to find a way to stop it.

"When is 17 November planning to do this operation?" Grimaldi asked.

"From what I gathered, they were pushed for time. Realistically, they could try as early as tonight."

"Then we've got to get there first."

"How?" she asked.

Grimaldi smiled. "On wings of eagles."

Portsmouth, England

A COLD, MISTY FOG shrouded the lights of the parking area around the Wellsboro Company printing factory.

Bolan and Mette watched from the cab of a panel truck, studying the quiet surroundings with interest. They had hardly spoken a word to each other since their arrival in England. One of Helonas's connections had arranged to fly the team directly into the airport at Portsmouth. The Executioner had to admit he was impressed with 17 November's resources. They had fingers into a lot of pies near and far, and quite a bit of support in both matériel and logistics.

The trucks were waiting at the airport. Mette rode with Bolan, and Jason accompanied Helonas in the truck taking up the rear. Other than Bolan and Helonas, nobody really knew what they were going to steal or where—just how. The Executioner wanted it that way, and he'd convinced Helonas secrecy was best. So other than those two, nobody had the faintest idea what had brought 17 November to England.

Their plan called for part of Helonas's group to set up a perimeter while Bolan took his team inside the warehouse. The remainder in the second truck not assigned to security would assist in the loading operation once Bolan's team identified the weapons and got them outside. They'd have to do this by daisy-chain effect, and that was going to prove equally advantageous in the Executioner's real plan.

A good part of 17 November—perhaps all if fate smiled on the warrior—would die tonight. Nonetheless, there wasn't a huge margin for error on this one. He had to find a way to take out most of the inside team while making it look as though someone else had done it. A firefight in the dark would disorient the better part of them. They'd make mistakes, work against one another and shoot one another. And then all the Executioner had to do was just get out of the way.

Bolan had used role camouflage before to penetrate organizations both large and small, and with a certain amount of success. It was simply a matter of tactics; making himself look like what his enemy wanted to see. It had worked time and again and proved once and for all that his enemies, be they terrorists, Mafia criminals or drug dealers, were inherently the same when it came to trusting their intuitions. They were usually pretty good at weeding out traitors among their midst—but Bolan was infinitely better.

"Have you wondered, Michalis," Mette asked, "if there was something beyond this?"

The Executioner looked sharply at the youth. "What do you mean?"

"If there's something beyond what we're doing here. A more peaceful life."

"I don't know," he replied with a shrug, looking through the windshield at the darkness. He wasn't sure if Mette was trying to bait him or not, but the young man seemed serious enough. "I've been around this sort of thing all of my life. I imagine there are better lives we could live, but it just wasn't the hand we were dealt."

"I have many times wondered if there weren't something better for me," Mette said quietly, a faraway glint in his eyes. "I joined 17 November while still in college. Jason convinced me that we could do a lot more for our people here than at the university, although I now have some doubts. I don't see how this is going to benefit my people. I don't see how my presence here will make a difference for Greece."

The Executioner was a little stunned by what he was hearing. He wondered if the path he'd chosen hadn't finally corrupted his ability to see the good in others. Perhaps he'd judged Mette too harshly. He was still a young man, and the way he was talking right now signaled a glimmer of hope. And perhaps, yeah, it was just possible that Helonas hadn't completely brainwashed this particular young man.

"Every man has to choose his own path," Bolan said. "Your path may not be the same as that selected for the rest of us. It's a part of destiny, Mette. And only you can decide your destiny if you really try."

"I will remember your words, Michalis."

Bolan raised the microphone of a shortwave radio to his lips and whispered, "Let's move."

He clicked off and then looked sternly at Mette. "In ten minutes, you have that truck by the door. Hear me?"

Mette nodded. "I got it, Michalis. Good luck."

Bolan nodded and climbed down from the cab. He began to whisper orders, indicating the team should fan out as they spread into a line about thirty yards apart, and then crossed the expanse together on a direct course for the warehouse.

The Executioner was wearing black fatigues and boots. He had an HK53 submachine gun slung across his chest, and the Beretta in his fist. Several fragmentation grenades were inside a tie-down bandolier, and the Desert Eagle and the 93-R rode in their customary spots.

They reached the warehouse within a minute and Bolan called in two scouts to work the door. He turned to look back at the second truck. Helonas's people were out and already setting up a perimeter. Good. They'd be far enough out that the Executioner knew he wouldn't have to worry about them getting in his way. Six were providing security, so if things got hairy and they retreated, it wouldn't be enough to worry about retaliation.

The majority were going down tonight.

The pair of scouts had the door open in seconds using a portable acetylene torch. They moved inside, followed by Bolan, sweeping the interior with weapons. The Executioner wasn't really sure what to look for. There were a hell of a lot crates inside there, and time wasn't a luxury he could afford.

Hyde-Baker had indicated the crates would be stamped as machine parts for United Kingdom Press. It wasn't much to go on, but it was what he had. The fact Wellsboro Company was a printing factory that stored machine parts for many presses didn't help matters any. It would be like trying to find a needle in a haystack.

Bolan gathered his group together near a metal stairwell that led to a maze of catwalks above the factory floor.

"We don't have a lot of time," he said. "I'll be watching you from above. When you've found the right crates, raise your hand and I'll get to you. Whatever you do, keep it quiet. Any questions?"

They all shook their heads in unison.

"Do it."

The group spread out and began inspecting the crates as Bolan climbed the stairs and alighted on the catwalk above. He could barely see them in the darkness, which was just fine. That meant they wouldn't be able to see him, either. He holstered the Beretta and traded it for the HK53. He'd wait until the crates were found and they started to load them before he'd implement part two of the plan.

Nearly fifteen minutes passed before the walkie-talkie on his belt suddenly crackled for attention. Bolan pulled it from his belt. "Yeah?"

"What is taking so long?" Helonas inquired. "We cannot stay out here forever."

"We're still looking for the crates," Bolan told him impatiently. Before shutting off the receiver he added, "Don't break radio silence again."

The movement of a hand nearby suddenly caught his eye. Bolan waved back to indicate he saw the signal, then quickly descended the catwalk and made his way through the maze of stacked crates until he reached the signaler. The man who'd found them played a penlight across the crate. Reddish-brown lettering was etched into the side: Mach. Parts, UK Press.

"That's it," Bolan said. "Get the others."

The man nodded and went to get the rest of the crew as Bolan pulled the radio from his belt and whispered, "We found them. Move in."

There was a burst of static in the radio, which was immediately followed by the roar of the truck engines starting. Helonas started to reply but then he was cut off.

And then Bolan heard the first echoes of gunfire.

Bolan tensed for action, bringing the HK53 into ready mode.

As he thumbed the selector switch to full-auto, two men from his team rounded the corner. The Executioner didn't waste any time telling them he was no longer an ally. The pair cast wide-eyed stares as they tried to bring their weapons into play.

Bolan's finger was already tightening around the trigger as he squeezed off the first volley. The 5.56 NATO slugs ripped through the first guy's chest, punching holes out his back before it slammed him against one of the crates. The second guy dived for cover, but Bolan simply tracked the muzzle with him, spitting another set of six bullets at the cyclic rate of 700 per minute. The guy let out a death scream before his head blew apart under the onslaught.

The soldier was on the move in a heartbeat, rounding the corner in time to see three more of his team running in his direction. This trio was even less prepared for the Executioner. Two fell under well-placed shots, but the third managed to find cover behind one of the crates. Bolan sought his own shelter from the steady stream of rounds the guy unleashed from a Zastava M-85 SMG. The cartridges it fired were identical to those in the HK53, but the guy wasn't nearly as proficient with his weapon as Bolan was with the HK.

The soldier waited until the guy had emptied his magazine and then rushed the position before he had a chance to reload. Surprise spread across the man's features, disappearing a moment later under the short burst of autofire from the Executioner's weapon. The man's head was vaporized at that range, and his corpse toppled backward onto the concrete floor.

Bolan pressed onward through the warehouse, looking for more of the 17 November terrorists. He didn't know what was going on outside, but that wasn't the pressing issue at the moment. Whoever had busted in on their party, Bolan ventured to guess Taylor was behind it. He hadn't intended for her to send the cavalry, but she thought she was helping him and he couldn't fault her for that.

Well, it was the diversion he'd needed, so he wasn't about to look a gift horse in the mouth.

Bolan found five other team members pressed against various crates near the door, and Thais was one of them. The terrorist widow was actually peering through the doorway, obviously trying to figure out what was going on outside. Factoring in the five he'd already dropped, this evened the count to ten—the last of his team were conveniently clustered together.

"Well?" he shouted, gesturing at them with his weapon. "Get the hell out there and help them! Our people are in trouble!"

"What was all that shooting?" Thais asked.

"A couple of cops, I think," Bolan lied. "They took us by surprise, but we managed to stop them. Now get out there and quit asking stupid questions!"

The team members nodded their assent and turned toward the door, bunching themselves together as if they were inviting the Executioner to mow them down.

He didn't waste any time in leveling the HK53 in their direction and obliging them. Firing those cartridges from a 210 mm barrel demanded one hell of a flash suppressor, and that's where the Heckler & Koch designers hadn't let him down. The group fell under the barrage of rounds, and in the darkness it took some time before they could figure out it was Bolan delivering them.

Three had fallen under the merciless onslaught before the remaining two split away from each other and sought cover. Bolan circled on their flank, changing out clips on the run. He moved through the warehouse like a ghostly wraith, and the terrorists were a second behind him as they raked the area with autofire from their M-85s.

Bolan reached the catwalk and ascended the stairs, triggering his weapon as he gained the high ground. Thais was one of the surviving pair. She tried to avoid the gunfire, but there was no escaping the Executioner's marksmanship. Three rounds took her in the chest, spinning her into a position where she caught two more in the back before toppling to the ground. Her life had ended as suddenly and violently as her husband's.

The last man managed to mark Bolan's position and readjusted his sights for the catwalk. A shower of sparks accompanied the hot lead that ricocheted off the metal of the catwalk or burned close past Bolan's neck. The soldier spun on his heel, ducking as he snap-aimed the HK53 and sent a fresh volley to keep the man's head down.

Bolan sprang to his feet and continued to the end of the catwalk. A fresh hail of gunfire nipped at his heels, and the Executioner decided it was time to put an end to the action. He yanked one of the incendiary grenades from his harness, snatched the pin and tossed the bomb over the side. It exploded a moment later in a flash of superheated gas, showering the lone terrorist with white-hot flames.

The man screamed in agony, a human torch that jumped from his spot and began to run in circles. Bolan sent a few mercy rounds at the flames, and the guy dropped like a stone.

The doors of the warehouse suddenly opened and a score of black-clad men entered the warehouse. They tracked the immediate area with their weapons, surprised by the embers of the burning corpse that lay directly in their path.

Bolan's eyes narrowed as he went prone on the catwalk and studied the new arrivals. A flash of recognition went through his mind and he suddenly realized he'd seen these men before. The body armor, the calculated movements, the silhouettes of MP-5 SD-3's. Yeah, no question about it—he recognized them because he'd worked with them many times before. There was no mistaking it. He now knew what he was dealing with, and it bothered him that he had to find out this way.

Mack Bolan was certain he was facing the SAS.

"NO, TELL THEM to stop!" Taylor shouted into the cellular phone as Jack Grimaldi steered her old, beat-up TR-6 toward the wharves at Portsmouth.

She shook her head with frustration and then looked at the phone before slamming it back into the cradle. "They hung up on me, those bastards! Can you believe it?"

"What did they say?" Grimaldi asked.

"They said I don't have authorization to stop the bloody raid," she replied. "Can't you push this thing any faster?"

Grimaldi looked at her in amazement. "Hey, it's a Triumph, okay? Let's not make it out to be a jet or anything."

Taylor's eyes narrowed but she smiled. "I happen to like this car."

"Whatever. How far to the wharf?"

"I'm guessing a few minutes," she said. "I had to call in some major favors back in London to find out where these weapons were. I hope it wasn't in vain."

"I just hope Mike's still alive."

"What's his story anyway, Jack?" Taylor asked pointedly. "He seems different from most men I know."

"He is different from most men," Grimaldi replied with a smile. "As a matter of fact, I'd say I've probably never met any man like him."

"How so?"

"He's cut from a different cloth than me or you. He's been doing this a long time. Sarge knows how to take care of business. He's put down a lot of bad people in his time, and I imagine he'll probably still be putting them down after we're both dead. At least in spirit."

"Do you believe in reincarnation?" Taylor ventured.

Grimaldi looked hard at her a moment and finally said, "I don't know. Do you believe in death incarnate?"

"I didn't think so until that other night in my apartment. When I saw Belasko in real action for the first time."

"Exactly right," Grimaldi shot back.

IT WAS GETTING crowded in the warehouse and that wasn't good.

Bolan decided it was time to make a hasty exit before he was discovered. He could still hear the sounds of battle going on outside. Seventeen November was putting up a hell of a fight, and Bolan wanted the SAS to know he was on their side. He couldn't get them to believe that lying there on the catwalk. It was time to take some decisive action.

Bolan jumped to his feet and spun to face a large window about eight feet from the catwalk. It was framed by thin strips of wood running both vertically and horizontally, and the glass didn't look all that tough. The soldier looked up and noticed a large hook dangling by heavy ropes almost straight ahead. He risked a glance back when he heard shouts and immediately saw the team of SAS commandos rushing his position, weapons trained on him.

Bolan slung his HK53 and then vaulted onto the catwalk railing. He jumped into midair and latched on to the hook attached to the pulley. The thing moved on a track that terminated close to the window. Bolan swung his legs forward as he reached the hook, and his weight began to set the pulley in motion. It slid along the track, gaining speed with each foot.

The Executioner crashed through the thin glass even as the SAS troops began to fire on his position. He sailed downward, expecting to see the unforgiving macadam rushing toward him, but instead was greeted by a four-foot-deep pool that stretched nearly the length of the warehouse. He splashed down and allowed himself to roll beneath the stagnant, murky water to absorb the impact.

A moment later, he was up and over the side of the trough.

A quick inspection told him the pool was a resource area for water used to cool the presses. Several large pipes protruded from the pool and converged on the side of the warehouse exterior.

Bolan quickly checked the action of the HK53 on the run as he made for the edge of the wharf. He could hear shouts of warning, and one man was yelling for him to stop and surrender in a multitude of languages. He figured the pier was his best bet in escaping detection by the majority of the SAS team.

As he continued toward the piers, the numbers began to run down in his head. And something didn't make a bit of sense here. He hadn't found time to tell Taylor what his plans were; perhaps she'd already known the weapons were in Portsmouth. However, that would have taken quite a bit of insight on her part to figure out 17 November planned to steal the L3A.

It seemed damn unlikely she'd have access to that information. It had nothing to do with her assignment in Greece—not in any direct sense anyway. There was a new game afoot here, and the Executioner was betting not all of the players had shown their hands. Well, it was still early in the game.

One thing was certain—he would have to bow out of 17 November. There was no way he could return at some later point and have Helonas and the others accept him into the fold. Too much wanton destruction had been rained upon them since his inception into the group, including the deaths of several key members.

Bolan knew Helonas would find that to be too much of a coincidence. The ruse was up, and now the Executioner was going to have to take 17 November on more direct terms.

As he reached the pier, he heard the squeal of tires on the pavement. He turned in time to see a small TR-6 Triumph skew to a halt twenty yards from his position. He raised the HK53, his finger tightening on the trigger, but he backed off when he heard the familiar voice of none other than Jack Grimaldi.

"You okay, Sarge?"

"Yeah," he said, trotting to the vehicle. "Right on time as usual, Jack."

He leaped into the back area, seating himself on the rear with his feet coming down into the small cargo space behind the seats.

Taylor flashed him a dazzling smile as Grimaldi powered the Triumph into a one-eighty and powered away from the pier. There was very little chance the SAS would catch him now, but if any of his pursuers saw the car they would have the British police put out a bulletin on it.

"What happened back there?" Taylor asked.

"You tell me," Bolan replied, fighting to be heard above the wind that cooled his sweat-stained face as Grimaldi accelerated the little sports car.

"I don't know what you're talking about," she countered.

"Oh, no? That was Special Air Service back there," he snapped, jerking his thumb behind them. "You telling me you didn't send them?"

"No, I swear. As a matter of fact, I tried to stop them."

"We're not sure who's at fault on this one, Sarge," Grimaldi broke in.

The Executioner cast a stare of disbelief at his friend. "What do you mean?"

"It's a long story," Grimaldi muttered.

THE MIDPRICED HOTEL in central London wasn't the best place, but it was fairly anonymous and probably the last place the police—or anybody else—would look for Bolan.

Not that Mack Bolan was hiding. They ditched the Triumph in the garage of Taylor's south-side condominium, traded it for a four-door sedan she also owned, and now sat at a table over the meal plates brought up by room service. It was well past midnight, and Taylor served coffee as they discussed their options.

"I talked to Hal while you were downstairs," Bolan told Grimaldi. "He tells me they never alerted the British about the L3As because of the potential risks it posed to me."

"Then that rules out our part in getting the SAS involved."

Bolan nodded.

"Well," Taylor interjected, "I certainly didn't tell them. It took every trick up my sleeve just to find out where the raid would take place. Jack's my witness on that bloody mess."

"She's right, Sarge."

Bolan shook his head. "Something's wrong here. These were SAS commandos, I'm sure of it. They moved like them and used the same weapons."

"Now that doesn't make any sense," Taylor replied. "The SAS can't operate within the country without express permission, except in times of war. They wouldn't have the authority to raid that warehouse unless they had the okay from government officials."

"Which means," the soldier concluded, "they probably did."

"Is it possible this is a rogue outfit here?" Grimaldi inquired. "Some group trying to look like the real thing?"

"It's possible but not likely." Bolan looked at Taylor. "Who has authority to implement the SAS?"

"They fall under the jurisdiction of the Ministry of Defence, as they're a branch of the British armed forces. However, there are select squads that can be assigned to special duties in affiliation with almost any branch under the PM."

"And that would include MI-6?"

Taylor nodded. "Yes. However, they can only be activated on authority from the PM or higher-ups within the Cabinet of War."

"Well, somebody tipped them off about the L3As," Bolan said. "There were only three people I know who had access to that information. Me, Helonas and Midas. Any bets on who tipped off the SAS?"

"Either one of them could have told our people," Taylor replied, "although I'm guessing it was Midas."

"Yeah," Bolan said. "And I'd be willing to bet he told somebody within the Greek government."

"You said something earlier about a connection between the Greek authorities and 17 November," Grimaldi said. "What's that about?"

"One of the major players in the group is the son of Nemo

Amphionides." He looked at Taylor and added, "That's the guy you met last night."

"Who's Amphionides?" Grimaldi asked.

"Deputy justice minister," Taylor explained. "He's a popular man with an influential family and lots of money. Not to mention one of the biggest politicians I've ever met. His boss has been taking quite a bit of heat from both the British and Greek parliaments for their failure to apprehend anyone within the 17 November organization."

"Everyone appears to know they exist," Bolan added. "The problem isn't knowledge, it's action and the will to use it. That's something I plan to remedy." There was a new fire in his icy blue eyes.

Grimaldi knew that look and asked, "What's your plan, Sarge?"

"The first thing I need to do is get Undersecretary Hyde-Baker out of that hellhole." He looked at Taylor and continued, "Which means I'm going to need the full cooperation of MI-6 and the Greeks. Any thoughts on who might be able to help us with that?"

Taylor nodded and rose from the table. "Let me ring up my supervisor. If anybody will help us, he will. I know it."

"Yeah, but can we trust him?"

"We can trust him."

With that, Taylor disappeared into the bedroom, leaving the two men to sit at the table.

Grimaldi and Bolan ceased their small talk as Taylor reappeared from the bedroom. There was just the hint of redness in the cheeks of her otherwise pale complexion. The Executioner could tell she'd been crying, and he knew that signaled really bad news.

"What's wrong?" Bolan asked, every sense on the alert.

"Sir Brygmart," she whispered slowly, choking back a fresh burst of sobbing. "He was found this morning in his home in Greece. Somebody shot him through the back of the head."

She looked up at the Executioner now as fresh tears fell from her cheeks. Bolan could really feel for her. He knew what it was like to lose those you worked with—sometimes even fought beside—and how really harsh it could be. He knew that this would affect Taylor for some time.

"They have no idea who did it," she finally managed to blurt out. She tightened up her fists and said, "Some bloody coward sneaked up behind him and killed him."

"Somebody's running around killing high-ranking members of MI-6 now?" Grimaldi asked Bolan. "What the hell is going on here, Sarge?"

Before he could reply, a grenade crashed through the hotel window, bounced across the floor and rolled to a stop within inches of the Executioner's foot.

Bolan kicked the grenade away.

The soldier clamped his hands over his ears, turned his eyes away and opened his mouth wide. Taylor was milliseconds behind him, obviously realizing it was a flash-bang grenade. Grimaldi didn't move quite as fast, and although he got his hands to his ears he didn't turn fast enough to avoid catching some of the concussion and the bright flash.

The pilot landed on his knees, but it took only a second for the Executioner to go to his side. Bolan hauled the Stony Man pilot to his feet, insured he was all right and then handed him off to Taylor.

A second grenade now came through the window, this one billowing smoke. As a gray haze poured from the grenade, Bolan immediately recognized the stinging, eye-tearing scent of CS gas even before it began to cloud the room.

"Help him out of here," Bolan snapped.

"What about you?"

"You just worry about Jack," he told her. "I'll worry about me."

Before they could do much else, several human shapes crashed through the window, attached to ropes. They landed feet first and fanned out, swinging the muzzles of Steyr TMPs into action. They weren't wearing body armor or fatigues this time, only protective masks.

Bolan already had the Desert Eagle out and sighted on his first target, backing toward the door to shield Taylor and Grimaldi while they made their escape. He took careful aim and squeezed the trigger. The weapon's report was nearly as deafening as the flash-bang. The crack and boom resounded through the hotel room, and the bullet smashed through the windpipe of the nearest gunman.

The other two opened up with the Steyrs.

The Executioner dived to the thin carpet and rolled, coming up on one knee and taking cover behind a wall. He braced his forearms against a corner post and fired the .44 Magnum pistol in a two-handed grip. The weapon thundered with each shot, adding a psychological edge to the Executioner's expert marksmanship.

One of the slugs punched a dime-sized hole through the stomach of one hardman and blew a fist-sized hole out his back, just above a kidney. The haze was now dense, and tears began to cloud Bolan's vision. There was only one enemy remaining, and he couldn't take the risk the guy might shoot him in the back or catch up to his friends.

Bolan holstered the Desert Eagle and traded it for his Colt Combat knife. He plunged into the heavy cloud of tear gas and charged his opponent. The move was completely unorthodox, and that was what the Executioner was counting on. While his enemy's mask would protect him from the effects of the gas, it wouldn't help him to see any better than Bolan could.

If his attackers had been smart, they would have launched the gas canister and then waited outside the front door to time their assault. This little tactical error cost them three of their personnel. Whoever was heading up this operation was probably not all that intelligent.

Bolan quickly found his opponent, who was crouched down and probably waiting for the Executioner to reload and start shooting again. He was on him before the guy knew what had happened.

The soldier reached out and grabbed one of the straps that tightened the mask. He pulled hard, yanking downward as he stepped in close to his opponent. The maneuver threw the man off balance, and the Executioner jammed the knife blade deep into a point at the base of his skull. The tip sheared the spinal cord in two and the man dropped to the ground, all nerve responses to his brain instantly severed.

Gasping and choking on his own saliva, Bolan beat a hasty retreat from the hotel room. He was careful to keep his hands away from his eyes, forcing them to stay open so they could tear. His throat and nostrils burned from the toxic effects of the CS gas. The gas formulated on the skin and soft tissues as crystals, and rubbing at them or pouring water on them only made it worse.

Bolan descended the stairs as quickly as he could manage and soon reached the ground floor. Two London police officers raced into the lobby as he hit the landing. The soldier slipped into an alcove beneath the stairs to escape detection. Once he was able to get past the lobby, the Executioner continued to the parking garage beneath the hotel.

He quickly located the car and Taylor already had the engine of the sedan warmed. She sat behind the wheel and Bolan gestured for her to slide over. The woman seemed agitated but did as he instructed without protest. Bolan looked into the back seat where Grimaldi lay on his side.

"You all right, pal?" the Executioner asked with concern.

"Fine," Grimaldi replied wearily. "Just a bit disoriented, that's all. And I'm still seeing some white dots in front of my eyes. I'll be okay."

Bolan nodded, put the sedan in gear and got out of there.

They pulled onto the street even as fire engines and rescue crews began to arrive. The sheer panic would cover their escape from the regular authorities, but Bolan didn't believe the enemy wouldn't pursue them. His concerns were validated when about a minute after the policeman waved them past the mayhem, a pair of headlights swung into place in the rearview mirror.

The Executioner was positively stymied at that point. There was very little intelligence that would explain the events of the past seventy-two hours, and he was beginning to think he was fighting a war on two fronts. He had really felt as if someone had been watching him since first boarding the train to Pátrai. The similarities between the team there and at the warehouse were uncanny, yet somehow the two groups were different.

Someone was manipulating the situation here; it was time to find out who.

"Someone's following us," Bolan declared finally.

Professional that she was, Dina Taylor didn't turn. Instead, she reached up to the visor, pulled it down and opened the cover to the vanity mirror. She tossed and scrunched her hair as if adjusting it, while checking out the bright reflection of the headlights. After about a minute, she eased the visor into place and turned to look at Bolan.

"It's too dark to really make out details. How long have they been on our tail?"

"Since we left town," Bolan replied.

"Can you make out how many, Sarge?" Grimaldi asked from the back seat, obviously feeling better now judging by the edge in his voice.

Bolan shook his head. "I'm not sure, but when I saw the silhouettes from the lights of a car behind it, I'd guess there are four. Dina, is there a good winding road around here?"

She nodded. "As a matter of fact, yes. About three miles from here is the road that goes through the government arboretum. It's open twenty-four, seven and a bloody nice ride, too."

"I'm feeling like a need for a good-old fashioned Sunday drive," Grimaldi cracked. "Can we go, Daddy?"

"Consider it done," Bolan said.

Within five minutes they had reached the road that went through the arboretum. It was actually just the kind of place Bolan had in mind—perfect for what he was planning. He ordered Taylor to get one hand on the wheel and steer for him as he double-checked the loads in the Desert Eagle and Beretta.

"When we get to the next corner, I'm going to bail," he told her. "Keep going for another minute and then circle around."

"What are you going to do, Sarge?" Grimaldi asked.

"Get some answers," Bolan said before opening the door and rolling away from the vehicle.

He could hear the roar of the engine fade away as he shoulder rolled out of the impact and got to his feet. The Executioner made for some high brush on the side of the road just as the pursuit vehicle rounded the corner. They had extinguished their lights, which was smart on their part. They weren't counting on the fact Mack Bolan was just a little smarter.

The soldier brought the Beretta into play as the sedan rolled past. He got to one knee, sighted quickly on the front tire and squeezed the trigger. There was a loud pop as the tire blew out.

The driver brought the vehicle to a halt and climbed out to inspect the tire. He looked at the back and front, and then immediately saw the damage. He said something in British-accented English, directing his voice to an unseen person in the back seat. There was a muffled but snappy reply before the rear door opened, revealing another man.

Two targets had now presented themselves, and Bolan knew he wouldn't get a better advantage. Yeah, there was no time like the present and the Executioner meant to get serious with his enemies.

Bolan raised his pistol and stormed from the bushes, taking the man who had emerged from the rear of the sedan. He stuck the muzzle of the Beretta against the back of the guy's neck and clamped a hand on his shoulder. The man froze and raised his hands; the soldier reached into his jacket and relieved him of his pistol.

The pair on the passenger side of the car jumped out, drawing pistols even as the squealing of tires signified the return of two more players. The driver had whirled toward Bolan, and now he redirected his attention to Taylor's sedan. Bolan's allies jumped from the car and drew on the group. It looked like they had a standoff.

"Put your pistol down, sir," the leader of the quartet ordered

Bolan. "You presently have a government official hostage. That's punishable by death here, you know."

Taylor suddenly lowered her weapon and squinted at them. "Kenley, is that you?"

The man turned to see Taylor. "Well, I'll be—" he began, and then he lowered his weapon and rushed to her.

The two embraced warmly and Bolan now had to admit he was really disturbed by this whole thing, although he realized these weren't hostiles. He released his viselike hold on the guy's shoulder and holstered his pistol. After a brief exchange between Taylor and the man she'd called Kenley, there was a sense of relaxation and everyone seemed a bit friendlier. Bolan returned the pistol to the man they called Butrick.

"What's going on?" the Executioner asked.

"Mike Belasko," Taylor said, "meet Kenley Godforth. He was my training officer in MI-6."

"And a bloody good recruit she was, mate," Godforth replied, shaking Bolan's hand.

"I'm sure," the Executioner replied, "but what I'd like to know is why MI-6 is following us."

"We're investigating the assassination of Sir Radley Brygmart, Belasko," Godforth replied, "and we're bloody well not the least bit interested in you."

"Don't be hard on him," Taylor told him. "He saved my life, and he's the only one who knows where Undersecretary Hyde-Baker is being held. He was assigned by the U.S. government to help us."

"Although it would seem they don't want my help," Bolan said. "At least they keep sending the SAS after me."

"That's because somebody tipped them off," Godforth replied quickly. "But the attack at the hotel wasn't the SAS, and it had nothing to do with you."

"What do you mean?" Grimaldi asked.

Godforth jerked his head in Bolan's direction before looking at Taylor. "Belasko wasn't their target, Dina. You were."

THE SAFEHOUSE USED by MI-6 was on the outskirts of London, away from the hustle and bustle of daily life. It was more like a cottage than a house really, and in other circumstances it would have spun homey feelings of warmth and security. Nonetheless, it presently held an isolated and eerie environment, feelings to which the Executioner was hardly unaccustomed.

Bolan, Taylor and Grimaldi sat at a table with Godforth and Butrick. The other two men were posted on guard duty outside, with an additional patrol roving on the nearby roads that led to the place.

Godforth was in the process of explaining their presence and his narrative was proving to be an eye-opener for Bolan.

"We've known about the association between Sir Brygmart and Nemo Amphionides for some time now," Godforth said. "But we hadn't done anything about it because we wanted to see where it went. The money Sir Brygmart thought he was stashing away was actually going right back into MI-6 coffers for distribution. We had his accountant by the scrotum, and we were squeezing for all it was worth."

"Cooperation in return for amnesty?" Taylor ventured.

"Something like that," Godforth admitted with a slight shrug. "We just didn't know it would go this far."

"Did you know that Amphionides is related to a prominent member of 17 November?" Bolan asked.

Godforth shook his head. "No idea. How did you find that out?"

"I've been working inside the group," Bolan said. "The man's name is Cyril Helonas. You might want to run that name by your people and check it out."

Godforth displayed an agreeable expression, and then turned and looked at Butrick, who nodded and excused himself.

"We'll see what we can come up with," he said.

"But in the meantime?" Bolan pressed.

"There is no meantime," Godforth said with an indifferent shrug. "It's out of our hands now."

"What do you mean?" Grimaldi piped up. "You just heard Dina tell you that Belasko knows where Hyde-Baker is. Aren't you going to do anything to get her out?"

"My bosses," Godforth said, tapping the table with his finger for emphasis, "have told me I don't go anywhere near Greece. Especially not this close to the conference. My job is to investigate the murder of Sir Brygmart—" he gestured to Taylor "—and to protect Dina until we can pin down the source of all this."

"Listen, guy," Bolan cut in quietly, something hard flashing in his blue eyes, "I understand your hands may be tied by the ignorant. I have no such limitations. I won't stand by and watch one more suffer because nobody wants to get their hands caught in the cookie jar."

"I have to admit that I'm with Mike on this one, Kenley," Taylor added.

"What?" he replied. "But Dina, he's—"

"Maybe," Taylor interrupted him, "but the life of one of our people is at stake here, and I happen to think that he's right. It won't do the conference a bit of good if they eliminate her. The undersecretary has been a key player in this thing."

"Nemo Amphionides doesn't give a bloody damn about that conference," Godforth argued, "and neither does most of the Greek cabinet for that matter. They'll go forward with their plans to destroy the conference whether or not they have the L3As to do it. And that won't solve the problem of the people who are trying to eliminate you."

"You keep saying that, but you haven't told me who this mysterious group is," Taylor shot back with a challenging stare.

Godforth reached up to a counter behind his chair and retrieved a large envelope. He dumped the contents on the table and sifted through them until he came to a large color still of a ruggedly handsome man with tightly shaved brown hair, a thick neck and dark eyes.

Taylor gasped as she looked at the picture.

"What is it?" Bolan asked.

"That's him!" she retorted. "That's the same guy who was in charge of those bastards you took out at my place."

"The one you called Zeus?"

"Yes."

"Except that's just his cover name," Godforth told them. "His real name is Lennox Barone. Origin and date of birth unknown."

"Who is he?" Taylor queried.

"Freelance assassin. We think that he's responsible for the death of Sir Brygmart, and we're fairly certain it's his men who are trying to kill you."

"That's no secret," Bolan said. "They've been trying to kill her since she was in Greece. As a matter of fact, this all started right after I infiltrated 17 November."

Godforth nodded. "It was Amphionides who let it leak into the organization that there was a mole in their midst. That probably had this Helonas hopping along with the rest of the group. It put them on edge and that made them dangerous to Amphionides. We knew that Sir Brygmart had several meetings with someone inside the Greek government, but it was only recently that we discovered it was Amphionides."

"So the deputy justice minister is involved in a conspiracy with 17 November to destroy the conference," Bolan concluded.

"That's what we think, yes."

"But why? What's the motive?"

"That's something we haven't determined."

"Maybe you're not looking in the right place," the Executioner pointed out.

His comment seemed to set Godforth's teeth on edge, but Bolan didn't really give a damn. This whole thing was outside of his league anyway. He was a soldier, not some Ivy League spy with an obsession for conspiracy. While he needed allies like Godforth—and he could only gain that alliance through Taylor—he also didn't have time to play tiddlywinks with the British government.

"And what would extensive experience lead you to conclude here, Belasko, eh?" Godforth snapped.

"Cut the sarcasm," Bolan countered. "We're on the same

side, remember? I'd suggest you look at this from another angle. Seventeen November's entire purpose here has been to discredit this conference. Everything they've done to this point is centered around that."

"So? What's your point?"

"Amphionides is obviously pulling the strings here. He wants to protect his own hide and achieve his own goals, be it power or money or whatever. I'd even be willing to bet he was the one that tipped off the SAS."

"Oh, come on, now," Godforth retorted. "Isn't that a little weak?"

"Ask yourself what motivates terrorists. Is it glory or any of this other stuff?"

"I think I understand what he's getting at," Taylor interjected. "Terrorists work solely for the propagation of terror or to achieve political ends."

"Right," Bolan replied.

He looked at Godforth and added, "I've worked side by side with Cyril Helonas. He considers himself a patriot."

"So what are you suggesting?"

"I'm suggesting we play this out," the Executioner said simply. "Put the lambs before the slaughter, play out enough to give them the smell of blood, then nail the lid on the coffin."

"And just how do you propose to do that, Belasko?" Godforth snorted. "You're not a one-man army."

Grimaldi stuck up a finger. "Could I comment on that?"

The Executioner just smiled at the ace Stony Man pilot's wit. "I have a plan."

Constitution Square, Athens

Mack Bolan cradled the Accuracy International L-96 A-1 sniping rifle—aka the Covert PM—as he sat atop the Alcmaeon Building.

His position afforded the Executioner a perfect view of the parliament building across the street. The pair of field binoculars near his feet had revealed six security positions, and he could see them from his vantage point but they wouldn't be aware of him. His selection of this position, thanks to the maps of Athens provided by Godforth's MI-6 connections, had been a careful one.

If there was anything Bolan didn't need, it was some overzealous security officer shooting him in the back.

The public announcement had been made only hours ago, and dawn had come and gone. Television crews were present, as was the press, and vehicles had been arriving for some time.

The conference was set to start at 0900 hours, and the Executioner was ready.

Bolan was certain that Helonas and 17 November would come; it was only a matter of time. They would come to destroy this conference for many of the same reasons that Bolan had come to stop them. They would do it out of a sense of duty, wreaking wanton violence and destruction whenever it suited their evil purposes.

But the Executioner had a much different agenda for 17 November, and it was going to start with a bit of military magic. Bolan had big plans for the terrorist outfit, including their first dose of the Bolan Effect.

The first sign of trouble was already beginning to show. Several people on the edge of the crowd to one side of the square were shooting off firecrackers. A couple actually had pistols and were firing them into the air.

Bolan set the sniper rifle in a position where he could get off the most shots in the least amount of time and then swept the crowd with the binoculars. Security was already moving in, and he didn't see any real threat. They were mostly protesters, and it would have appeared from the magnification that they were holding nothing more than starter pistols.

Bolan swept the field glasses to another point, a break between two of the buildings. The entrance to the alleyway was only about twenty yards from the front steps of the parliament building, and the Executioner had immediately marked it as a trouble spot. Nothing had appeared yet, however, and he rechecked his sight alignments and took a deep breath.

Taylor and Godforth had set up a security detachment inside the building at the entrance. The stay instituted against Taylor by the foreign secretary had been lifted, thanks to some hard evidence provided by Godforth that pointed to Brygmart's collusion with sympathizers inside the Greek cabinet.

However, that was all circumstantial evidence. The case against Nemo Amphionides remained pretty thin, and there was no way they could have him removed from office until they were better able to prove his affiliation with Helonas and this Lennox Barone.

The man who called himself Zeus was another problem that weighed heavily in the Executioner's mind. Who was Barone working for, and what did that have to do with 17 November?

The first attack against them aboard the train had probably been engineered by Amphionides—the Executioner was convinced of that. The late MI-6 chief had obviously utilized the deputy minister's people to throw the hounds off his scent.

That meant Brygmart had seen the writing on the wall. He'd become fearful of his position in this conspiracy, anybody could see that. But afraid of whom? Helonas maybe? That didn't wash, which left only Amphionides. So that meant Amphionides might have arranged for Brygmart's assassination. It wasn't anybody within 17 November—that didn't fit. And it certainly wasn't an act Bolan could picture Amphionides would dirty his own hands with. Was it possible that this was where Barone fit in?

There were really only three major players left here. Amphionides, whose allegiance was to himself; Helonas, whose allegiance was to 17 November; and Barone, whose allegiance was anybody's guess.

Nonetheless, Bolan knew it was only a matter of time before he would encounter Barone again. He'd let British and Greek officials take care of Amphionides. When his job was done here, he'd move on to the remnants of 17 November, including Helonas, and that would conclude his mission.

The flash of light on metal caught his eye and he immediately brought the rifle into the action. Through the powerful scope the Executioner saw three terrorists emerge from the alleyway. He couldn't repress a smile, satisfied that if 17 November continued to act with complete predictability it would make his job much easier.

Bolan sighted on the first terrorist in line through the Schmidt & Bender scope, leading him just slightly and making a slight drop adjustment before stroking the retooled trigger.

The 7.62 mm projectile exited the rifle with a muzzle velocity of over 800 meters per second. It slammed through the gunman's chest and blew out a lung, continuing through the back side of the body before it lodged into the wall behind him, visible to Bolan by a marking of dust that flew through the air.

The guy twitched in death throes, visible in the scope even as his colleague behind him stopped and looked around. The pair of terrorists had obviously set their sights on murdering whatever diplomat had just pulled up in the Mercedes, but it wasn't going to happen this day. Or any day for that matter. The next few seconds would be their final ones.

Bolan brought the bolt forward, took a half breath and squeezed the trigger for a second time. The bullet crossed the expanse with blinding accuracy and ripped out his throat. Blood spurted openly from an artery, showering its hot contents on the dying man's comrade.

The Executioner watched the terrorist sink to his knees next to the last target even as he stroked the trigger.

Security officers were still running around the immediate crowd, pushing back bystanders even as complete pandemonium shook that area of the square.

Bolan edged away from the sight and looked around. He quickly spotted something going on at a building that was much lower than his and at a right angle. He leaned back to the telescopic sight and swiveled the barrel to face that direction. He saw one of the security people succumb to pistol shots in the back.

Two terrorists—one carrying the pistol and the other what looked like an RPG launcher—stepped over the body and made their way to the open precipice. They were going to fire a rocket into the square! The terrorist carrying the RPG knelt and aimed the launcher toward the crowd pressed against the immediate area next to where Bolan had dropped the three terrorists. They were obviously convinced the shooter was inside the crowd.

Bolan realigned his sights in that fatal instant, focused on the launcher-toting terrorist and squeezed the trigger twice. The first 7.62 NATO round went through his stomach. The round sheared off part of the diaphragm, kidney and liver before exiting the other side. The second punched through the forward port, pushing the RPG down and toward the roof.

The immediate area where they stood erupted into a bright

orange ball of flame, and incinerated the two would-be killers. The impact from the round had done the job the Executioner hoped, causing a misfiring of the RPG. It was a fitting end to two animals who would have killed hundreds just to eliminate one possible opponent.

Before Bolan could adjust his position further, an object sailing through midair caught his peripheral vision. He turned just as an explosion rocked the rooftop where he was positioned and sent him toppling over the edge.

NEMO AMPHIONIDES watched the street below from his office in the parliament headquarters with a mixture of amazement and disillusion.

Someone was making a complete fool out of 17 November, and this was further troubling because they were making a complete fool out of him, as well. His plans hinged on the success of Cyril and the group to shut down the conference, which was scheduled to begin within the hour. The problems in the street were certainly going to slow down the process, but it would hardly intimidate the hard-nosed members of NATO's subcommittee.

They continued to arrive in Athens like clockwork. A few minutes ago he had received word that even now the few remaining members had arrived at the airport and would be present for the conference in less than thirty minutes. And it didn't appear the situation was improving any. Perhaps the panic and violence among the citizens in the streets would frighten the dignitaries into a postponement of the conference. That would give Amphionides enough time to make his play for power.

Then again, it looked as if most of the casualties—if not all of them—were on the side of 17 November. Amphionides didn't know who was behind the slaughter taking place below, but he could venture an educated guess. It was probably the man they called Belasko.

He'd heard through Midas of the failed attack on the warehouse and also of the American agent's disappearance. There hadn't been any further contact with Zeus since the elimination of that imbecile, Brygmart. That meant the British woman with MI-6 was still running around loose somewhere.

Well, the deputy justice minister of Greece wasn't about to put up with any more of this nonsense. It was time to establish order down there, and he'd pull strings with the PM or the security people to disperse the crowd and shut down this entire conference.

Amphionides whirled on his heel and left his office. He walked down the carpeted hallway, his three-hundred-dollar shoes slapping the floor through the thin carpet. He reached the service stairs in the front corner of the building and descended purposefully. Yes, he would take care of those animals on the streets and the whole operation would fit perfectly into his plans.

The DJM pushed through the door that led to the great hall that was actually considered a lobby. He saw the security people checking everyone who came in, and he could still hear the mad roaring of the crowd outside. He'd call in the military if it meant he could preserve some sort of order. Then everyone would see that he was much more qualified to lead the country than this present band of simpletons.

Amphionides froze in his tracks when he spotted a short, well-built woman with blond hair. She was dressed in civilian clothing, but she was brusquely inspecting the face of every person who passed through the portable security system set up under the orders of the Justice minister. He knew that face because he'd seen the dossier on her.

It was the Taylor woman! And she was right here inside the building!

Amphionides suddenly didn't feel well—a queasy sensation rolled over him. It turned his stomach, and he thought for a moment he might retch. He turned immediately to prevent the British agent from seeing his face. Zeus was supposed to have taken care of this little problem, and he hadn't even done that. One woman!

This was becoming more aggravating by the moment. Amphionides immediately retreated to the landing inside the stairwell and braced himself against the railing until the nausea passed. The situation was out of control, and he now had to do something.

Suddenly, it occurred to him. He would simply turn his own people against Taylor. If he could convince them she was a security risk, considering the present situation outside, his men would most likely take her into custody and ask questions later. At least it would buy him the additional time he needed to see his plan came to fruition.

Amphionides climbed the stairs and went to his office. He smiled to himself even as he picked up the telephone to make the call. This would be a time long remembered, for it had seen the end of one British spy, and it would soon see the fall of another.

THE EXECUTIONER HUNG from the ledge by one hand.

Muscles strained against the flannel shirt he wore, threatening to tear the sleeves from broad shoulders. Years of combat had hardened Bolan's body and mind, and given him the catlike reflexes that had saved his life on countless occasions.

This was one of those times.

From a lower rooftop on the adjoining building, somebody had fired a HE grenade. Blood flowed freely from a jagged laceration in Bolan's forearm, but he ignored the pain. This wasn't time to lick his wounds. Whoever had fired that projectile probably had more than one. They had also figured out his position somehow, and that troubled him immensely. He'd been extra-cautious to conceal himself from security. Not that he suspected his attacker belonged to the Greek law-enforcement detachment.

The Executioner slowly and agonizingly pulled himself up over the parapet and soon regained the rooftop. He rolled to one knee, leaving the rifle in place and bringing up his Beretta 93-R in a two-handed grip as he thumbed the selector switch to 3-round bursts. He scanned the precipice on the west side of the building, which tapered off to the adjoining structure two stories lower.

No threat presented itself, so Bolan got to his feet and sprinted to the edge. He caught sight of the tall, muscular figure running toward the far side of the building. It was hard to discern features from that distance, but as the man turned and looked in his direction there was little doubt in the Executioner's mind that he was looking at none other than Lennox Barone.

The assassin raised something even as Bolan snap-aimed the Beretta and tried for the long-distance shot. The two men squeezed the triggers of their respective weapons simultaneously. It was a rather large weapon that Barone fired, probably a Magnum version judging by the report. It was only a single shot compared to Bolan's three.

The heavy round from Barone's weapon sent dust and stone chips flying harmlessly past Bolan as the Executioner's rounds nipped at the assassin's heels. Bolan fired another trio of 9 mm Parabellum rounds and one appeared to graze Barone's leg. The man staggered, fell, rose and fell again, finally getting to his feet and reaching the rooftop access door.

The Executioner holstered his weapon and dropped the five-plus yards to the roof below. He hit easily, rolling through the jump and coming to his feet on the run. He reached the doorway and pulled it wide open, the Beretta in his fist again as he swept the interior. It was considerably darker inside, poorly lit in comparison to the morning sun climbing higher in the sky.

Bolan took the stairs two at a time but watched the areas ahead of him with great caution. It was unlikely Barone would stop to spring an ambush, wounded as he was, but Bolan wasn't taking any chances. The guy had proved quite resourceful before, and the Executioner hadn't lived this long by being reckless.

He continued down the stairs, stopping on occasion to listen for the footfalls of his quarry. Bolan could hear the grunts of pain and struggling breath echo up to him in the stairwell. He continued descending the steps and soon arrived in the lobby. Just as he reached the landing he saw Barone plow through the front revolving door of the building.

Bolan sprinted after him as Barone passed beyond the doorway, entering the crowd outside. The Executioner continued onward, pressing forth in his pursuit of the mysterious assassin like a hunter chasing an elusive fox. The guy was really nothing more than a wounded animal, and he would fight back with the same ferocity if cornered.

The soldier pushed through the glass doors with his two-hundred pounds of sinew and muscle, coming up short on the sidewalk to keep from knocking down a young woman. He looked around and caught a glimpse of Barone as the assassin moved through the crowd. Bolan continued the pursuit, skip-breathing to keep himself from becoming too winded with the chase.

His quarry couldn't run forever, and the Executioner knew that this was going to end soon. Barone reached an alleyway and turned into it, followed a moment later by Bolan. The alley terminated at a set of stairs that dropped down to a doorway. It was a common feature of building access in Greece, and the Executioner knew his enemy had nowhere else to go.

Barone had to kick at the door several times for it to give in, and Bolan quickly closed the gap. The assassin was barely inside when the Executioner descended several steps, braced his hand on the top one and launched a side kick that connected with Barone's spine. The assassin was knocked into the dark, dusty interior by the harsh attack, the wind exploding from his lungs with a wheeze.

"Party's over," Bolan growled.

Barone spit a small dribble of blood from a split lip, an injury he'd obviously gotten in the fall. Bolan stood over him, reached down to grab his collar and hauled him to his feet. The assassin rammed a knee into Bolan's groin, missing his testicles by inches but landing hard on the inner thigh.

The Executioner twisted away from the unexpected maneuver, whipping an elbow up to impact under Barone's chin. The guy was staggered by the blow but he stayed on his feet. Bolan launched an undercut to the guy's stomach, contacting two lower ribs and cracking them with the blow.

Barone grunted with the attack but managed to land a haymaker against Bolan's left cheekbone. The Executioner's teeth jarred together and his head snapped to the side. The guy hit fast and hard, and Bolan knew he'd have to end this quickly.

The soldier lowered his center of gravity, turning sideways as he drove the heel of his boot to the inside of Barone's shin bone. The blow was enough to fracture the tibia, sending a sliver of bone poking through the skin. Barone roared in pain, reaching for his pistol as he staggered backward.

The Executioner stepped sideways, using the heel of his left palm to redirect the barrel of the pistol. Barone only got off one shot before Bolan broke the bridge of his nose with a rigid blow from a forearm strike. Blood squirted everywhere even as he grabbed the wrist of Barone's gun arm, stepped inward and under the arm, and twisted it back and away. The wrist snapped under downward pressure and Barone screamed with further agony.

The screams died in his throat when Bolan shoved his face against a 50-penny nail protruding from a wooden post. The head was missing and the thick, rusted spike punched through Barone's skull and penetrated his brain. Something bordering on a mixture of surprise and pain filled Barone's face. Then he coughed his last breath. The light left his eyes and he just hung there from the nail, his eyes and mouth wide open.

The issue of Lennox Barone—aka Zeus—was closed.

As Bolan turned to leave he whispered, "One down, two to go."

Cyril Helonas watched with sadness from deep within the throng that clamored outside parliament.

Someone had gunned down five of his people before they could take out even so much as one diplomat. The terrorist realized that his world was falling apart here, and there was little doubt left in his mind that 17 November was doomed to fail on this front.

Part of his animosity was directed at his own people. They sat there like simple and uneducated savages, waving signs in either protest or support. The citizens of Greece couldn't even come to an agreement on whether they wanted this thing. It seemed more like a demonstration just for demonstration's sake than any real statement. Eliminating those enemies of Greece who would attempt to interfere in Greek affairs was the only true, decisive course of action. Standing in Constitution Square, screaming and shouting at the top of their voices wasn't a way to solve any problems.

What angered him most was that his father sat poised on some self-made throne inside that very building, probably watching the festivities at that moment with smug satisfaction.

Helonas wouldn't have admitted it to anyone but he missed Michalis. He wondered what had become of his friend after the raid. There was a possibility that this comrade-in-arms had fallen under the guns of the SAS—like so many of their people had—unable to escape the vicious ambush set for them. Nonetheless, he didn't want to accept that possibility, and he had it on good sources that Michalis's body wasn't among the dead at the warehouse.

That meant there was an off chance Michalis Belapoulos was alive, and if he returned he would be able to tell Helonas what had happened. Helonas wouldn't accept the fact Michalis might have been behind the raid. Mette had told Helonas that Michalis took the team inside and that before they could even get the crates out, the SAS had stormed the area.

So that left really two scenarios. One, Michalis was alive and lying low for a while, keeping his head down and naturally wanting to get back to 17 November. Two, Michalis was dead. He could never believe his friend had betrayed him. Midas's information was either bad, or it wasn't Michalis who was the traitor in their midst. There had to be another explanation.

Either way, Helonas wasn't just going to stand there and wait for some answers. He was going to get them right from the source. It was time to see his father.

Helonas crossed the square, pushing through the massive cloister of bodies until he reached the front entrance. He held up an envelope and waved it at one of the security officers who supervised several subordinates covering that part of the crowd with machine pistols. A handful of people pressed his legs hard against the barricade, and Helonas cursed to himself, trying to keep his balance while not flipping over the heavy iron gate.

"Excuse me, Officer!" Helonas yelled, struggling to be heard over the demonstrators. "I must get through! I have information here that is vital to the security of the conference! I must see the deputy justice minister!"

"Whom do you wish to see?" the officer said, stepping past his men and approaching Helonas cautiously with one hand on his pistol belt.

"Nemo Amphionides, deputy justice minister of the cabinet."

"And what's this information?" the officer countered. "Something perhaps resembling a bomb or such?"

"No, I am an official courier. The deputy justice minister knows me by name. Tell him that Cyril is here with information."

"Why not just pass it over to me?" the officer suggested, interested now in the envelope Helonas waved as he held out his hand. "I will make sure the deputy justice minister gets it."

Helonas shook his head. "I cannot, I'm sorry. I was given strict instructions to deliver this only to Minister Amphionides. Please..." Helonas looked around him and added, "I implore you to let me through."

"All right," he said, stepping back behind his men again and waving for Helonas to step under the barricades. "But no tricks, mind you, or I'll order you shot down here and now."

"I am not deceiving you," Helonas added as he crouched under the steel works and moved into the area now contained by the security forces. "I am unarmed."

Helonas raised his hands and waited patiently for the officer to have one of his men search the terrorist. When the policeman confirmed Helonas wasn't carrying a hidden weapon, the security leader gestured for him to follow. Helonas couldn't repress a smile of satisfaction when the officer turned his back. This was going to be easier than he thought. Sometimes the Greek law-enforcement officers could be so mindless.

No, careless was a better word for it.

They passed through the front doorways and the security officer took Helonas to one of the metal detectors. He passed the envelope off to the right as he walked through. He got on the other side and saw one of the officers opening the material. Helonas snatched the envelope from him before he could get the seal fully broken.

"What are you doing, you fool?" Helonas snapped. "You can't open that. It's information only for the eyes of the Ministry of Justice. Even I am not privy to its contents. Are you trying to get me imprisoned?"

Before the officer could say another word, a middle-aged

man in a three-piece suit approached them and put up his hands to draw attention. "What's going on here?" he asked.

He had a British accent and Helonas looked him in the eye. "I am a special courier to the Ministry of Justice. I have documents here for the deputy justice minister, Nemo Amphionides. They are sealed and this dolt—" he gestured to the guard "—was trying to inspect the contents."

"All packages and briefcases must be inspected, sir," the man replied with a cool smile.

"On whose authority?" Helonas challenged.

"The prime minister, of course," the British agent replied.

"National security of this nation supersedes that," Helonas insisted, clutching the envelope filled with empty sheets of paper close to his breast. "I insist on seeing the deputy justice minister and allowing him to decide that."

"I'm afraid—"

There was a commotion at the other checkpoint on the far side of the vestibule. All eyes turned in that direction as several uniformed soldiers suddenly surrounded a short, blond-haired woman.

Helonas's eyes popped open with surprise as he immediately recognized the beautiful features. It was Diona Crysanthos—and members of the elite police unit were shackling her while Helonas's father looked on. The man who had come over to them now rushed to her aid, putting an immediate stop to the arrest, waving his arms and demanding to know what the hell was going on.

There was something very strange here, and it seemed even more so for Helonas.

He hadn't seen his father in person for nearly five years, and the sight of his own flesh and blood caused his blood to run cold. He'd always looked up to his father, respected him, and he could never understand how someone from his own family could betray the cause of the Greek citizenry—especially in his position as DJM.

That's why Helonas had opted to drop his surname, and retain only his first and middle names. It was a way of shedding ownership. He'd told his father that he disowned him and that he would never set foot in his house again. But this was different—it was purely business. And no matter how Helonas might have felt about his father's political views, he knew one thing with assurance.

Nemo Amphionides wasn't the kind of man who would sell out his own family; Helonas believed that with every fiber of his being.

But that wasn't the issue that preoccupied his mind at the moment. It was seeing his father's men arrest Diona Crysanthos. He had to do something to save her, but he was one man—a wanted terrorist—against a score of armed security police. The really troublesome thing was the fact they were arresting her. Were they trying to get to Michalis, using her as the bait?

"What's going on?" the male Briton asked, pushing some of the guards away.

"This woman is a security risk," Amphionides insisted. "She's under arrest."

"What the hell are you talking about, mate?" her counterpart asked. "She's a member of the security team."

"She's part of the sympathizers who tried to blow up the diplomatic headquarters in Pátrai and a traitor," Amphionides insisted.

"What?"

"Oh, yes. I have it on good authority that she was seen there trying to create a diversion while her people set the bombs." He turned his attention to the guards and said, "Take her away and if this man interferes you may arrest him, as well."

"You can't do this," the man responded.

"I'm sure that I can," Amphionides replied, turning on his heel and marching away.

The guy started to walk after him, but several guards intervened and favored him with looks of warning as they made a show of reaching for their side arms.

"My government will not take this lightly, mate!" the man hollered after Amphionides.

"You may take it up with my superiors by appointment. In

the meantime, I am acting on the authority of the prime minister for the duration of the...emergency."

The whole incident had taken less than a minute, and Helonas was actually dumbfounded by the whole thing. He knew he should have been moving toward his father but he didn't want to risk Diona seeing him. The most astounding fact was that his father seemed convinced—at least from the conversation—that Diona had something to do with the attack on the building in Pátrai.

Other than the fact that she had gotten the explosives for them, there was no connection. Witnesses claimed that they had seen her trying to create a distraction in Pátrai? She hadn't been anywhere near that building when it exploded. Or had she? There were a lot of unanswered questions, and Helonas had to find out what was going on.

The officer who had escorted him to the building ran after Amphionides. "Deputy minister?" he called.

Amphionides stopped in his tracks and waited for the officer to approach. The two men had a whispered exchange and then the officer pointed at Helonas. Amphionides looked at him, flashed a mixed expression of surprise and recognition and then nodded and whispered something to the officer. The security guy came back to Helonas and indicated for the terrorist to follow him.

Helonas walked after the man as he watched Diona led away in handcuffs.

"EVERYTHING LOOKS GOOD up here, Sarge," Grimaldi's voice said through the earpiece.

The ace pilot was now airborne, circling the area with the Gulfstream C-21A jet high above the clouds. Even at a ceiling of forty-five thousand feet, Grimaldi could see a dime on the sidewalk with the advanced observation equipment aboard. This was proving invaluable, but once they had landed at the Olympic Airport it had taken some time for Grimaldi to get off the ground again.

That was too bad because Bolan could have definitely used him earlier to watch his back.

The two men were communicating over a high-tech radio linked to Aaron Kurtzman's new satellite communications system. His invention had quickly earned the reputation of being reliable and invaluable in operations such as these. Phoenix Force and Able Team had field tested the system through the worst of circumstances, and it outperformed expectations every time.

The scrambled communications were transported by digital relays. The information was processed in binary code that secured 128-bit encryption, and was further filtered on various frequencies that alternated every five seconds. Whether the information was sent by voice, facsimile, shortwave or electronically made no difference. The system enhanced information communications, bringing it to a superior level and using hardware not available to any private or corporate organization.

Kurtzman had worked with some of the finest minds in the world, each applying his or her specialty. Graduates from MIT—as well as electronics experts in Russia, Europe and Japan—had all contributed one piece to the final project, so anybody who'd worked on the thing didn't really have a clue what they were doing, which cut the security risks to almost nothing.

It was Kurtzman who had wrapped the whole thing together using computer software he'd written personally. The Stony Man crew affectionately referred to the communications system as the "Bear phone."

"Sounds good, Jack," Bolan replied.

"Okay," Grimaldi retorted. "We can set—"

"Jack, you there?"

"Yeah, but something's coming through over one of the security frequencies." Bolan could hear the worried tone in his friend's voice. "Uh-oh, you're not gonna like this."

"What's up?" the Executioner asked as he moved toward Parliament headquarters.

"Sounds like they arrested Taylor."

"What?" Bolan said, starting into a trot for the building.

There was a long pause and the soldier waited patiently for Grimaldi to send an update. There was no point in haranguing the guy. He'd get the intelligence to the Executioner as soon as possible.

"Actually, I'm getting a lot of radio activity," Grimaldi finally said. "I just talked to Godforth over the secure line. I guess Amphionides has taken charge of the security measures. He's alleging Taylor had something to do with the bombing in Pátrai, and that she's a security threat."

"Sounds like Amphionides is covering his tracks," Bolan replied. "Tell Godforth I'm on my way."

Grimaldi signaled he understood and then signed off.

The Executioner was sprinting now. He vaulted the steel barricade in a single bound and headed up the steps. Many of the protesters were beginning to disperse, probably out of fear of getting shot like the 17 November terrorists. The soldier wasn't interested in them if they weren't interested in spreading havoc. The local authorities could handle any rioters.

Several of the security men shouted for Bolan to stop, raising their weapons to gun him down when he refused. Godforth met him at the door and waved the group away, warning them that Bolan was on their side. The Executioner pushed through the doors, walking toward the security office with purpose even as Godforth rushed to keep in step and spit out a breathless explanation.

"Why didn't you tell them who she was?" Bolan asked.

"Amphionides wouldn't let me. He ordered his men to arrest me if I interfered. Claimed he was acting under PM authority."

"He's acting under nobody's authority," the Executioner snapped.

"But he acted like the prime minister has declared martial law," Godforth argued.

Bolan looked hard at him and countered, "On the day of an antiterrorist conference between NATO and high-ranking members of the Greek government? Think about it. Amphionides is crooked and we all know it."

They reached the security office and Bolan burst through the front door. Taylor looked up, as did the four guards holding her prisoner. She was manacled to a chair at hands and feet. There were looks of surprise on all five faces, but more on the guards as Bolan walked around the processing counter and approached the senior man.

"Let her go," Bolan told the officer who wore the markings of a captain.

"What's the meaning of this?" the man demanded in an accent so heavy that they could hardly understand him.

"You're holding a British citizen illegally," Godforth ventured in an authoritative tone. "You have no right to detain her."

"We are under orders from the deputy justice minister," the officer barked.

The Executioner showed the man a cold smile and said tightly, "Those orders have been revoked."

"Under whose authority?" the officer snapped.

The Beretta was in Bolan's fist with lightning speed. He pulled the captain up against him, circled his neck with a rigid forearm and pressed the muzzle of the Beretta against his temple.

"Mine," Bolan said, gesturing with the pistol. He looked at one of the captain's underlings and said, "Release her right now."

The other three men looked at one another, and Godforth produced his pistol to cover them in case they thought they could outgun them. It was four-to-two odds but Bolan gave them a look that told them he considered those in his favor. With the exception of the captain, the officers were young and appeared limited in experience. They decided in that heartbeat that discretion was the better part of valor.

Bolan breathed a sigh of relief that they hadn't called his bluff. He would never have shot a law-enforcement officer, especially not one who was simply operating under the orders of a demented cretin like Amphionides. But he couldn't afford to have Taylor holed up somewhere in jail while he was trying to bring down a conspiracy bent on destroying the efforts to end terrorism in Greece.

As a matter of fact, at that moment he needed all the allies he could get.

The guards quickly disengaged the shackles from Taylor and returned her weapon to her. Bolan then disarmed each man and herded the quartet into a service closet. He locked the door from the outside with a skeleton key. It was one of the old-fashioned type doors carved from heavy wood. They wouldn't be able to break out easily, especially with all of them crammed in such a narrow space.

The trio quickly left the security office and emerged in the hallway.

"You two," Bolan told them, "better get a team together and go after Hyde-Baker. I'm sure they'll kill her as soon as they've figured out we're on to them. She won't have any further use and I've still got my hands full here." He told Taylor where she was located.

Taylor nodded. "We'll take care of it."

"Which way did Amphionides go?"

"Toward that stairwell," Godforth replied, gesturing to the far end of the corridor.

"Are you going after him?" Taylor asked.

"Yeah. It's time to end this little game of his once and for all." He turned to face Taylor and added, "By the way, your little problem with Zeus has been alleviated. Permanently."

"You killed Barone?" Godforth asked with surprise.

Bolan said, "He tried to blow me off the roof while I was sniping 17 November's hit team."

"But how did he know you'd be here?" Taylor asked.

"I think Amphionides had him shadowing me," Bolan replied. "As a matter of fact, I think Amphionides has been pulling the strings here from the beginning. He's the only one who we know is connected to all of the other players. It makes perfect sense and it supports my theory that there's a terrorist sympathizer inside the Greek government."

"But can you prove it, Belasko?" Godforth asked.

"I don't need to prove it," Bolan asked. "I'm not a judge or jury. I'm the judgment."

And with that, the Executioner turned and headed for the stairway.

Mack Bolan searched the second floor of the building, but saw no one.

The members of the subcommittee had arrived, and Bolan knew it wouldn't be long before Albertson got there. The Executioner saw the plans by the NATO subcommittee and the Sheringham Articles as a fresh chance for Greece. The war against terrorism was without end, which Bolan understood better than the average person did.

But there was more to this war than just fighting back against the Hydra that continued to rear its many heads. There was that ability to implement effective measures to prevent terrorist actions—it was that part of the war that governments and principalities would find difficult. They had to show a single front, make a united stand against the animals that blew up school buses and gunned down old women. And the problem was finding common ground to stand on where political viewpoints and philosophies could stay at the door.

When the politicians could do that with consistency, it would effectively put an end to terrorism. Until then, it would take men like Mack Bolan to make a difference in society.

Bolan was climbing the steps to the third floor when four men appeared at the top. There was no question that he'd seen this group before. They wore black fatigues and carried machine pistols—Steyr TMPs actually—and the situation all came together for the soldier in a blinding flash of realization. It was Amphionides who had been manipulating these men, using them not only against Bolan but also 17 November.

However, it didn't really matter at the moment because they were as surprised to see the Executioner as he was to see them—although that hadn't really cut down on their reaction time. They reached for the Steyrs slung at their sides, trying to find cover on the narrow landing.

Bolan had the Beretta out before the men could do much else. He thumbed the selector to 3-round bursts and unleashed two volleys at the group. Two of the rounds drilled through one man's chest, knocking him backward into his counterparts. The third round sailed above them and crashed through the window that lit the landing.

Two of the men were still trying to sidestep the first man's falling body when another fell under the second set of rounds. The subsonic 9 mm hollowpoint rounds splintered bone and splattered the wall with brain matter as they cleaved his skull like a trio of knives. The guy spun, his finger jerking on the trigger of the weapon.

One of the remaining pair managed to get the door open and dive through it while the other went prone and tried to gun the Executioner down. A series of 9 mm Parabellum rounds ripped out sections of wood on the ornate lamp that hung above Bolan's head as he ducked behind the door.

Bolan raised his weapon, sighting just above the Steyr that glinted in the morning light. The soldier squeezed off another three rounds, one tearing off the man's jaw, while the other two tore into his chest and traveled down to lodge in his intestines. The guy choked on a mouth full of blood, and it poured freely from him as his head dropped.

The last of Amphionides's minions had set up a firing position behind the door leading from the third-floor landing. He began to fire long bursts at Bolan, not really coming close enough to hit the Executioner but more to keep his head down.

During one of the moments of firing, Bolan dropped his clip and reloaded a fresh one, and then thumbed the selector to singles. This wasn't the time to be running out of ammunition, and although he'd still had more than a half-dozen rounds left in the old clip, Bolan didn't want to get caught with his pants down in the middle of a hot situation—much like the one he had going now.

There was a lull in the autofire as his adversary changed magazines, and Bolan decided to use the lapse to his advantage. He launched himself up the steps, firing on the run and forcing the guy to rear back behind the door frame before he could bring his TMP into battery.

Bolan got to the landing and dropped prone. The guy managed to get his Steyr working and brought his arm around the corner, raking the area above the Executioner's head with a deadly fusillade of 9 mm gunfire. The gunman then risked a glance around the corner and Bolan took his shot.

The round zipped a neat furrow in the side of the neck, but it wasn't enough to be permanently disabling. Bolan's opponent screamed, ducking back behind his cover as he dragged the Steyr with him. The warrior didn't wait for an invitation but got to his feet and rushed the guy's position. He charged around the corner and saw the man was running down a hallway, moving away from him as fast as he could.

He wouldn't be hard to track, as he was leaving a fairly large trail of blood. Bolan began to wonder if he'd nicked one of the veins or arteries in the neck. The Executioner continued to chase the gunman, who was rounding the far end of the hallway.

Bolan poured on the speed, executing a shoulder roll as he reached the end of the hallway and coming up on the far side with his pistol ready. No gunfire greeted him. He saw the guy lying facedown in the middle of the corridor, blood covering his clothes.

Bolan trotted to the body, flipping it over with his boot, the muzzle of the Beretta pointed at center mass in case the gunman was playing possum. The Executioner sucked in his breath, a little stunned at what he saw. It was a very young man—maybe eighteen, maybe twenty—with dark hair and lifeless brown eyes.

Bolan clenched his teeth as he lowered his side arm. The bullet had nicked the carotid artery and with the running the kid had lost blood quickly enough that it killed him. What Bolan found most disturbing was how young his opponent had been. Now it would seem that Amphionides was recruiting kids to do his dirty work.

It was time to find the man who was responsible for so much death and had caused so much pain and eliminate him once and for all.

Bolan continued his search.

FORMER CIA SECTION CHIEF Kermit Albertson nervously drummed his fingers on his knee as he sat in the back of the Mercedes.

When he'd agreed to serve as a witness for the NATO subcommittee, Albertson never envisioned it would be like this. He could have never foreseen during his service in the Company that he would one day have to spill his guts regarding the criminal activities and political espionage that seemed so prevalent in the Balkan states and Commonwealth of Independent States.

Albertson had seen quite a bit of horror and injustice in his career. Death abounded throughout many of these countries, and serious damage was being done internally. Although those facts might not have been all that visible to the outside, it didn't really matter. Albertson knew it existed, and nobody could have told him differently if they tried.

Particularly disturbing to the former government agent was the situation brewing right here in Greece. Athens—named after the goddess of wisdom, skills and warfare—was truly honoring its namesake. The Greeks resented the presence of foreign powers in their nation, if the crowds he'd seen in Constitution Square were any indication, and Albertson really didn't want any part of it.

The truth of the matter was that Albertson was here for himself, and that was that. He was divorced, had no children and lived a bit on the wild side of life. He had a house in Boca Raton, Florida, and a hacienda-style getaway tucked into the hills of central Mexico. Which was exactly where he planned on disappearing to after this fiasco was finished. Nobody knew about that small tidbit, a perk he'd acquired while serving as a field agent in the city of Torreón.

Yes, when this was finished he planned to disappear; they would never find him.

The driver eased the Mercedes through the throngs that beat and spit on the windows. The bulletproof glass rendered very little comfort to Albertson. Why the hell the police hadn't cleared these people out was anybody's guess. Moreover, Albertson was remiss to understand what had the natives so restless to begin with.

The NATO subcommittee was here to help the Greeks do something they obviously couldn't, or wouldn't, do for themselves. They were trying to end the terrorism in this country, and the people they were trying to protect only saw the invasion of their sovereignty and the imminent threat against what amounted to nothing more than a puppet government anyway.

So what did he care?

The driver guided the Mercedes to the back and pulled in front of the rear doors. Four security officers and two American agents waited there. Albertson didn't recognize either one of the fresh-faced pair, but their body language screamed "CIA" for a hundred miles.

Albertson climbed from the seat after the bald bruiser who'd escorted him from the airport got out and gave the all-clear signal.

The entourage proceeded inside the building, nobody speaking to Albertson. The police cleared the corridors while the two Company agents led the way, followed by Albertson, with the bodyguard bringing up the rear. To Albertson's way of thinking, this whole thing was pretty damn ridiculous. They were treating him like the President or something. The former spook couldn't see any rhyme or reason for all of this attention. Nobody even knew who was coming to "testify"—certainly nobody on the committee knew. Albertson just couldn't see what they were being so anal about.

The bodyguard knew only that he was a VIP, referring to him as Mr. K., which Albertson thought was about as corny as you could get. The two agents didn't know his name at all, and Albertson knew they were under strict orders not to speak to him other than where to stand, when to come or go and so forth. It was a real waste of manpower that could have been better spent somewhere else. Treating him like this made him less conspicuous.

What a group of morons!

One thing Albertson knew: when he was done with this little song and dance he'd be out of there and on his way to a new life.

And the sooner the better.

"YOU REALIZE, Cyril," Nemo Amphionides told his son quietly, "that if you are discovered here it means the end of your organization and your life. I will not be able to protect you."

"Perhaps, Father," Helonas replied with disdain, "but it does not really matter now. Thanks to your information, we know that someone is coming to blow the whistle on our operation. We cannot let that happen."

The two men were seated in Amphionides's office now, and Helonas had to admit he was impressed. When he'd decided to leave, his father was newly elected to the Ministry of Justice. It was this fact that actually drove the wedge between them, because Helonas believed his father had betrayed the people for his own political ambitions.

His cousin Midas was little more than a boot-licking follower, and would have supported Amphionides's views for as long as it suited his purposes. Helonas couldn't bring himself to that point of view. Right was right in the Greek terrorist's eyes, and he wouldn't compound the mistakes his father had made by supporting a form of government in which he didn't believe.

That was the biggest problem between father and son.

The familial ties were certainly strong, as with most Greek men, but Helonas found himself compelled to rebel against the outrages. The Greek parliament and executive offices wouldn't attempt to resist the political "invasion" of foreign powers, but Helonas fought for the people. He defended those who couldn't defend themselves, and he wasn't about to just stand by and do nothing while the politicians and traitors in the government sold Greece's independence to his sworn enemies.

"It won't happen," Amphionides replied in an assuring tone. "I already have someone in place to take care of the big-mouthed American."

Helonas couldn't suppress a scowl. "Oh, come now... I know you better than that, Father." He folded his arms in disgust and said, "Have you even identified this man yet?"

"No, but he is scheduled to arrive soon. Once I know who he is, I can arrange to have him silenced once and for all."

"I think that you should let me worry about that," Helonas offered. "You would not want anything to come back and spread ruination on all of your great plans. This is a dangerous time for you, Father."

Nemo Amphionides lent a coy smile to his rebellious child. "That's very considerate of you, Cyril, but I'm not the fool you might believe me to be. I know what you're trying to do, and it's not going to work."

"And what am I trying to do?"

"The last two operations mounted by your—" he paused and then continued "—people haven't exactly been the large successes you would have hoped."

"Certainly, my people have experienced a few setbacks recently. But that doesn't mean we will not reign victorious in the final analysis."

It was Amphionides's turn to snort in derision. "You call those setbacks? You have practically lost your entire operation in the past four days. Now you would try to convince me that you can recover from this?"

"One of my people did quite well to plan our operations,"

Helonas countered, adding a touch of vehemence to his voice. "Midas tells me that we have a traitor in our midst. It is that individual who has foiled our plans by disclosing them to foreign powers."

"Oh, you would be speaking perhaps of your half-breed friend who disappeared during your attempt to steal the L3As from Portsmouth?"

Helonas found himself speechless. He couldn't understand how his father would have known of the operation. Midas didn't know; only two people had known about the operation until its implementation. The terrorist immediately became suspicious of Michalis. Yet, that didn't make any sense. Was it possible that Michalis had been working for his father? Helonas considered the possibility and then quickly dismissed it. He knew the man well enough to know that he wouldn't have worked for a man like Nemo Amphionides.

There had to be more to this story.

"How did you know about that?" Helonas asked quietly.

"I have my sources," Amphionides snapped. "Sources much better suited for this kind of game than you might imagine."

"The woman that you arrested? She is Michalis's sister. What are you trying to hide, father?"

"That woman is not Michalis's sister, my son," Amphionides replied condescendingly, "and his name is not Michalis Belapoulos. It's a cover. He's an American agent by the name of Mike Belasko, and his sister is actually working for MI-6. They were assigned to rescue the Hyde-Baker woman. You've been duped!"

"How can you prove this?" Helonas asked. "I personally witnessed Michalis torture the British undersecretary. He was the one who extracted the information on the whereabouts of the L3A."

"Did you actually see him torture her?"

Helonas started to speak and then stopped himself, suddenly having to admit he hadn't actually seen Hyde-Baker confess to Michalis. Or was his name really Mike Belasko? Was it true, what his father had said? It certainly wouldn't have served any purpose for him to lie to Helonas, and the terrorist began to see the light. So it had been Belasko all this time, and he'd been too stupid to see it.

It all made sense now. Belasko and the British woman had arranged for the failure in Pátrai, as well as the attack by the SAS in Portsmouth. And now his so-called friend had disappeared—a disappearance that moments earlier had Helonas worried but now caused him only to be incensed.

"I feel like a fool," he finally said. "I was misled by this man, and drawn into befriending him out of loyalty for my people. He has not only betrayed me but he has betrayed 17 November." Helonas stood and snapped, "And that I can not forgive."

Amphionides raised his hand. "Now, wait a moment, Cyril."

"I will not wait, Father," Helonas replied, spinning on his heel and heading for the door. "This is my honor and the honor of 17 November at stake. I will make this Belasko pay for what he has done."

Helonas could feel the rage swelling within him as he walked toward the door. The man he had called his friend was now his sworn enemy. Before this was over, he would see Belasko dead. And if he couldn't destroy him, then he would make it his personal life's pursuit to hunt him down and kill him. Although he would make him suffer, perhaps implement the tricks Belasko had learned in Argentina—if he'd even been in Argentina.

All of the lies and the deceit rushed in on Helonas in that moment; he seethed with the thought that he was betrayed. Helonas considered the possibility that it was Belasko who had killed Endre and Guilio. Perhaps it was also Belasko who had murdered his people in the warehouse and brought down the wrath of the SAS. Yes, it all made perfect sense to him now.

When Helonas opened the door, his eyes widened with surprise. He found himself looking into the cold, icy gaze of his enemy.

The blow came so fast that Cyril Helonas didn't have time to deflect it.

Bolan delivered an uppercut that lifted the Greek terror-monger off his feet. He landed hard on his rear end, the back of his head clipping a chair and opening a small gash.

The Executioner stepped through the doorway, keeping one eye on the bleeding and disoriented Helonas as he eyed Amphionides with cold distaste.

"You're done here," Bolan said, drawing his Beretta and pointing it at the deputy justice minister. "It's men like you who poison this society. You claim you're working for your people, but you've actually sold them into fear and slavery. You accepted a bloody ransom to further your own goals."

Amphionides raised his hands but he was smirking.

Bolan knew the guy didn't give a damn about human life one way or another. The Executioner had met his kind a thousand times over. Men like Amphionides preyed on the innocent. They made a living spreading death and corruption throughout everything they touched, and all in the name of personal gain. It didn't matter to Amphionides how many people had died today because of him. All he cared about was himself, and his wants and desires. He was an angry, selfish man and Bolan had grown weary fighting against his devices.

"Killing me won't accomplish anything," Amphionides said. "My son here will simply carry on in my stead."

Helonas started to rise and Bolan favored him with a hard expression. "You can get up, but do it easy."

Helonas nodded and rose, then reached to the back of his head. He drew blood on his fingers and he stared at the Executioner with a renewed expression of hate and betrayal. Bolan wasn't bothered by the look. He'd been long prepared for the moment when he would face Helonas for the first time after the terrorist realized he'd been deceived.

"You ate with us, Michalis," Helonas said almost breathlessly, "or whatever your true name is. You slept among us, laughed with us. And through it all you arranged all of these mishaps and pretended to be ignorant."

"True, I had a lot to do with it," Bolan agreed. He gestured at Amphionides with the pistol. "But I didn't arrange all of the mishaps. The police officers who attacked us on the train? A little present from your father here. Not to mention it was him who told the SAS we were going to steal the L3As."

"That's ridiculous," Amphionides said. "How could I have known about that?"

"The same way you knew about everything else," Bolan snapped. "You engineered it."

"You have evidence of this?" Helonas asked.

"I don't need evidence. The British know that he was meeting with a member of MI-6. The meeting between you and I was arranged by him, as was the rumor of a traitor within 17 November. As a matter of fact, everything in these past few days was the result of his manipulation, and I think he used Midas as the mouthpiece."

"You may kill me if you want," Amphionides said, "but it doesn't really matter. We know about the rat who is here to tell the NATO subcommittee about collusion within my government. This person will be dead within the hour."

"Hardly," Bolan said.

He looked at Helonas. "Your old man has been using you, Cyril. Do you honestly think you came by all of the information you did on your own? He wanted you to kidnap Hyde-Baker so he could wash his hands of it. With her out of the way, there wouldn't be anything to stop him."

"No!" Helonas exclaimed. "I will not listen to you anymore. You are a liar and a traitor. I trusted you once and you destroyed that trust. I will not make that mistake again!"

Helonas leaped at the Executioner, taking him off guard. Bolan sidestepped the attack in time to prevent being overcome, but Helonas managed to get one hand wrapped around his right wrist. The two began to fight over the pistol, and Bolan cursed himself for letting the terrorist take him by surprise.

Helonas managed to knock the Beretta from Bolan's grip and rammed his head against the Executioner's solar plexus. Breath exploded from his lungs, threatening to drive him into unconsciousness. The gun was too far to reach now, and Bolan knew if he didn't end this that he wasn't going to get another shot. Helonas was still a killer, and he would take Bolan's life given half a chance.

The soldier drove his knee into Helonas's thigh, striking the nerves there hard enough to cause Helonas to loosen his grip on Bolan's wrist. He executed a hip toss and slammed Helonas to the ground. The terrorist was still partially stunned by Bolan's earlier offense, and this maneuver appeared to weaken him some.

The Executioner heard a bellow behind him and turned just in time to see Amphionides rushing him with a broadsword that had been hanging on the wall. Amphionides swung the sword in a horizontal slash, trying to lop off the warrior's head. Bolan ducked under the attempt and got to the opposite side of the blade.

Amphionides was older, but his grace and speed surprised Bolan. He quickly corrected the motion and swung the sword in an arc, intending to bring it crashing down on Bolan's skull. The Executioner rolled away from the move. He came to his feet and watched with surprise as the sword carved a large gouge in the wood beneath the thick carpeting.

Bolan dived for the pistol and came up in time to snap-aim the weapon. He almost fired at Amphionides, but movement in his peripheral vision caught his eye. He whirled and saw two more of Amphionides's men enter the room. They were both heavily armed with Zastava M-76 automatic rifles, and Bolan considered those the greater threat over a broadsword.

He squeezed the trigger twice, taking the first gunman high in the chest. The impact slammed the guy's back into the door frame, and he collapsed to the floor. Bolan was tracking on the second man as his target raised his rifle, but the round missed by mere inches as Amphionides jumped at Bolan's gun arm.

The Executioner twisted, bringing Amphionides with him, and rammed an elbow into his nose. He immediately followed up a rock-hard punch to the side of Amphionides's temple and then grabbed the guy by the hair. He slammed his face into his own desk and lifted Amphionides off the ground before the man could recover. With a mighty heave, Bolan hurled the murderer through the window, sending him sailing into midair amid a plethora of broken glass.

Automatic gunfire began to resound through the room as the other terrorist realized he no longer had to worry about hitting his master. Now it was just a matter of killing the invader. A volley of Mauser slugs hammered at the walls, windows and furniture as Bolan dived behind the desk for cover.

The Executioner waited until there was a lull in the shooting before coming out from behind the desk. The doorway was empty and he could no longer see his opponent. He swung his pistol into a ready position and set it to 3-round bursts. He looked over the desk to where he'd left Helonas.

The terrorist was gone! He'd probably slipped out while Amphionides's man kept Bolan occupied. The Executioner got to his feet and sprinted into the hallway. It was as if the pair had simply vanished into thin air. Helonas had escaped to plan his revenge. Bolan knew he was going to have to deal with the terrorist once and for all.

But first he had to get to Albertson. Once he'd eliminated the threat of anything happening to the CIA agent, he could concentrate on finishing his business with 17 November.

KERMIT ALBERTSON dropped the magazine he'd been skimming and stood when one of the Company guys walked through the door and nodded.

It was time for him to go perform his duty—such as it was—for the subcommittee and his country. Like he was about to buy that load of crap. At least that's what he'd kept telling himself to justify this whole, dumb matter. The magazine was written in Greek anyway, leaving Albertson to look at a rather drab collage of black-and-white photos. All he wanted to do was get this over with and split.

Albertson would sure be glad when he could complete his mission and move on with this thing. The nameless CIA agent escorting him turned and started to open the door, but it came a bit harder than either of the men were expecting. The escort backpedaled, running into Albertson and knocking both of the men on their butts.

The guy that stepped through the door looked like he meant business, and the pistol in his hand only served to strengthen that observation. Albertson's training took over and he immediately sized up his opponent. He was a big dude, probably six-two or -three, and even through the loose clothes Albertson could see the muscular physique. But it was the face that belied the real power. The jaw looked chiseled from granite, and the ice blue eyes stared at the two men without reservation or fear.

Albertson figured he was finished; he wasn't carrying a gun and he was fairly sure the Company guy wasn't, either. That left very little hope the pair would walk out of the situation alive. But something behind the grim visage staring at them wasn't completely lifeless. There was the faintest hint of a smile at the corners of the mouth, and something emanating from the guy left Albertson with the impression he was looking at somebody on their team.

"Which one of you is Albertson?" the man asked.

The escort immediately spoke up. "I am."

"Then I'm thinking it's really you," the guy replied instantly, gesturing the muzzle of his pistol at Albertson.

Albertson nodded, smiling at the man out of newfound respect. This guy was pretty sharp. "Yes, I'm Kermit Albertson."

"Good, now we're getting somewhere." The newcomer looked at his escort. "Who do you work for? CIA?"

The man didn't say anything and Albertson kicked him. "Speak up, fella. The guy's holding a gun."

"Yeah," the younger agent said hoarsely.

The man lowered his weapon and allowed them to get to their feet. "Then I'm on your side. What's your name?"

"Prevalucci," the Company guy replied quickly, "Tommy Prevalucci. And you are—?"

"The name's Belasko. I don't have a whole lot of time to explain, but suffice it to say that I'm here to protect Albertson." He looked at the former CIA spook. "Ever heard of 17 November?"

Albertson nodded. "Who hasn't? They're the biggest bunch of pain in the asses this country's ever generated, and they're elusive as hell."

"Not anymore. I'm here to punch their ticket. But the deputy justice minister had a nasty surprise planned for you in that conference. I don't know who the trigger man is, but I'm fairly certain he doesn't know who you are, either."

"The deputy justice minister of Greece?" Albertson asked with disbelief in his tone. "Are we talking about the same guy here? Nemo Amphionides?"

"Yeah, only he's the late Nemo Amphionides," the big guy replied. "Like I said, I'm certain the assassin doesn't know your name or what you even look like, especially since the subcommittee didn't. That's why I'm going to take your place."

"Say what?" Prevalucci bellowed. "You can't do that. There are escorts inside that chamber who do know who he is, and they're going to expect him to take the stand. They see anybody else and I guarantee they're going to shoot first and ask questions later, pal."

Belasko smiled. "That's why you're going to tell them not to worry and it's all part of the plan."

"Now look, buddy—"

"No, you look," Belasko said, shoving a finger in Prevalucci's face. "I don't have time to argue with you, so don't play tough guy with me. If Albertson shows his face in there he's dead. On the other hand, I stand a pretty good chance because I'll be ready for them."

"What if I could get you inside the chambers?" Prevalucci offered. "You could watch from nearby and nail this bastard when he makes his move."

The man patted the pistol he'd returned to a holster beneath his black leather jacket. "Wearing this? There's no way they'd let me inside there armed without the proper credentials, and we both know it. The only way I can make it inside is if I'm posing as Albertson. And you're going to help me do it."

"Fine," Prevalucci groaned, raising his hands and stepping back a pace from the towering visitor.

Albertson had to admit that he liked this idea pretty well, and he smiled widely at the big guy. If this got him a permanent reprieve, he could get out of here all that much sooner and forgo the ceremony. And the idea of Belasko putting his life on the line to spare Albertson made the plan seem all the better. How could he say no?

Bolan looked at Albertson now. "Once I've drawn this assassin out and concluded that business, you can get out there and do your stuff."

"But I thought—"

"I'm sure you did, but you don't get off the hook quite that easily, Albertson. You need to tell these people what you know. It's the only way to make things better."

"Do you honestly think," Albertson said, crossing his arms, "that what I have to tell that committee out there is going to make a damn bit of difference, Belasko?"

"I wouldn't be doing this now if I didn't think so," Bolan reminded him. "Look, Albertson, there comes a time when we all have to stand up for what's right. I'm not one for asking a man to do something he doesn't believe in, but at some point you have to decide to believe in something. Now, you can either go out there and try to help, or you can cower in the corner. It's your choice."

"I've never cowered from anything, mister," Albertson snapped.

"Then this is your chance to prove it," Belasko said easily. He smiled and added, "So let's make it count."

EVEN AS BOLAN ENTERED the chambers and noted the ten faces seated behind a long table, he couldn't help but feel apprehension. The room wasn't very big, which meant a shootout could risk a considerable number of lives. If possible, the Executioner knew he'd have to take this guy at close quarters, and he'd probably only get one chance.

Immediately behind the committee were several chairs arranged on a sort of dais resembling a jury box. Not every chair was filled, but there were a few people occupying them, possibly staff aides. One was a stenographer, and she sat patiently with her hands in her lap.

Several security officers were scattered throughout the room, along with a couple of men dressed in suits and ties. Probably CIA or special-assignment officers from the Greek police force. Any one of them could have been the assassin, as could any one of those members seated at the table. At this point of the game, nobody was above reproach for the Executioner.

Yeah, he would have to be watchful.

Prevalucci escorted him to a chair that faced the table, and Bolan sat. There were about six faces he didn't recognize, probably all members of the NATO subcommittee. Also seated at the table were members of the Greek cabinet, and he recognized them from the dossiers provided by Stony Man.

All the big-wigs were present, including the heads of the public order, justice and foreign ministries, as well as Balasi Pyramusakis, the New Democracy deputy who had recently gotten his mug splashed all over the papers for his radical views against foreign interference. There wasn't much doubt in Bolan's mind that Pyramusakis could be the trigger man, given his short stature and Napoleonic complex.

The minister of public order stood and opened the conference with a brief call to order and a wonderful speech about how they were gathered in the name of peace and in the hopes of establishing a new and safer democracy in Greece. He ranted about how the country had been subjugated to the tyranny of terrorists, and droned on about the apathy of the members of parliament.

Pyramusakis sat down at the conclusion of his speech, and then one of the members of the NATO subcommittee addressed Bolan.

"Please state your name, profession and business with this body today," the woman instructed him.

"My name is Kermit Albertson," Bolan replied evenly. "I am a former chief of the Balkan-states section for the Central Intelligence Agency, and I'm here today to testify against several key members of the Greek cabinet, who I personally can identify as sympathizers with the terrorist organization 17 November."

"And how did you come by this information?" one of the other NATO members asked.

Bolan said, "Because as a section chief I was in regular contact with these people. In many cases, I was responsible for setting up surveillance on them. I know they met with members of 17 November and I recorded many of their conversations."

"And are any of these people present now?" the man asked.

Bolan decided to take a shot in the dark. "Yes."

Almost as if on cue, one of the plainclothes Greek officers reached beneath his jacket and withdrew a pistol. He rushed forward, aiming his pistol at Bolan and firing repeatedly as he drew closer.

Confusion and excitement erupted throughout the room even as Bolan left his chair and dived for the floor. Rounds from the semiautomatic pistol zinged the air where he'd sat only milliseconds before. Bolan rolled to a kneeling position, the Beretta appearing in his fist, safety off and selector preset for 3-round bursts.

The Executioner unleashed an answer in that moment.

The Beretta let out a cough as the subsonic slugs rocketed on a true course for their target. All three rounds punched through the gunman's chest, driving him backward into the wall as his pistol flew from lifeless fingers. The guy was dead before he hit the ground and the assassination attempt was over before it had begun.

Several of the other officers rushed the gunman and turned him over, cuffing him even though it was obvious he was dead. The remaining few had rushed to protect the dignitaries, a couple drawing beads on Bolan as he rose to his feet and holstered his pistol.

"It's all right," he told the committee members as he turned and nodded thanks to Prevalucci.

That was two down...

Cyril Helonas was still reeling from the events of the past few hours.

The ultimate hatred and rage for Belasko burned his bowels, and he didn't know if there was anything—not even cold revenge—that would cool those embers. This man had betrayed him and taken everything important to his life. He'd murdered his friends and his father, and now it was almost certain he would come after Helonas.

That would be a battle Belasko wouldn't soon forget. Helonas was a skilled soldier and tactician in his own right. There were only a handful of members from the organization remaining, and they had sworn to fight to the death with Helonas. It would be interesting to see what Belasko planned to do against an army of well-trained revolutionaries instead of a group of unsuspecting incompetents.

In some respects, Helonas felt responsible for the deaths of so many of his friends and comrades. It was he who had entrusted the group to Belasko, and it was he who had refused to see the truth.

"Within hours, this madman who we knew as Michalis will come for us. He will not find us, however, because we will have moved to our backup quarters on Sikinos."

"Why don't we fight him here, Cyril?" Jason asked, looking at the rest of the group. "I realize that I am new to all of you, but I do not think we should turn in cowardice and run from this man. We have nothing to fear here."

Helonas stopped in front of Jason and put his hands on his shoulders. He admired the younger man for a moment, realizing how much Jason resembled him some years back. Many years back, when he was younger and much more idealistic. Years had passed since the assassination of Saunders, and Helonas had learned much since then. He didn't consider himself an eager-eyed zealot out to change the world as he once had.

"Exercising patience and good judgment is not a sign of cowardice." He looked to the other members and continued, "Right?"

They all nodded their approval.

Helonas looked Jason in the eye again. "This is a tactical withdrawal. It gives us time to draw Belasko into our trap."

"But he will have his own time to plan," Jason protested.

"Jason is right," Mette spoke up. "We must face this man here on our own terms and in our own city. To run would be a sign of weakness."

"This is a matter I think the group must vote on," Helonas offered, realizing he was losing control. While Jason and Mette were vibrant and courageous, they would still be more likely to go along with the group.

The rest of the members took a vote and decided that it was better for them to move to their base on the island of Sikinos. It was located about 150 miles south of the mainland, midway between Greece and Crete. It was neither terribly large nor populated, and they knew it was unlikely that anyone would find them there. Belasko didn't even know of the fortress.

"Well," Jason said, "I will not just run away from this. I don't know if anybody else wants to support me, but I will wait here for this man."

"The group has voted that we retreat to the island," Helonas reminded him. "It is not for you to decide for the rest of us. If you choose to stay, then you are choosing to forfeit your lot with 17 November."

"Is that the way you feel?" Jason asked him sarcastically.

"It is not about how I feel, Jason," the Greek terrorist reminded the smart-mouthed youngster. "These are the rules by which all of us agreed to abide."

"And they agreed to abide by your decision to trust the American," Jason shot back offensively. "It is a wonder all of us weren't destroyed."

Helonas hung his head and replied quietly, "The blood of many of our people is on my hands, true. Including that of my own family." He raised his head, looked at the group and added, "But this man killed my father. Hurled him from a window without feeling or remorse. I know his kind. He will not stop until he has destroyed all of us."

Many of them let out murmurs and nods of assent. Helonas then looked at Jason and said, "Do not throw your life away over some self-indulgent rationalization. You have neither the skills nor the experience to repel a man like Belasko. Let us work together for those ends. Believe me when I tell you that I want vengeance as much as you do. But let us do it in the correct manner."

Jason looked at Helonas for a long moment before nodding his head. "Very well, I will go with all of you to Sikinos. And when this Belasko comes I will crush him underfoot like so many of the rats that scurry by down here in these sewers."

Helonas smiled and the group left to make preparations for their departure.

"STAY ON THE LINE, ace," the Executioner told Jack Grimaldi.

"I'm with you, boss," came the pilot's reply.

Bolan picked up the telephone inside the security office. He was surrounded by a group of Greek police officers, but this time they were on his side. Bolan had told the justice minister and other members of the Greek cabinet about Amphionides and revealed all that had transpired within the past few hours. He had now been given a considerable amount of latitude and they had decided to postpone their session until Hyde-Baker was safely returned.

But that's when Bolan had received this phone call, and it was one he couldn't be completely sure was one he wanted until he heard the news.

It wasn't good. "Mike, this is Dina. We found the base of operations but 17 November is gone."

"And the undersecretary?"

"Gone, as well."

So Helonas had run from them, probably advising the members of the organization to do the same. But they had bothered to take Hyde-Baker with them, and that meant it wasn't over. A man like Helonas would seek revenge for the death of his father; the Executioner knew the terrorist well enough to deduce that. The retreat and the fact they took Hyde-Baker with them were almost challenges.

They always made their decisions as a group, which meant that they wouldn't have split up if they were holding a hostage. Obviously, they had another base of operations somewhere.

"Okay, Dina, I'll take it from here."

"Are you sure? You should really let us help, Mike. You've already done more than enough."

"No, this is as much a matter between me and Helonas as it is about rescuing the undersecretary and destroying 17 November. Helonas is sending me a message, and I'm going to give him the reply he's looking for."

"All right, but be extra careful."

"Count on it."

Bolan hung up and left the security office, rushing toward the back door where a sedan was waiting that had been provided at his disposal. The subcommittee and members of the Greek cabinet were definitely showing their gratitude for his interference in the conference, and for saving their lives. It was more public exposure than the Executioner would have preferred, but he hadn't been left with much choice.

There was no doubt in the Executioner's mind that 17 November had retreated to another base of operations, and it was likely that Helonas knew Bolan would come for him. The soldier wasn't stupid or naive, and he wasn't going to talk himself into believing that Helonas hadn't come to know some parts of his inner man. The time they had spent together had been close time, and no cover was completely devoid of some reality.

The basic ability to command himself and his tactical expertise would have shown through, not to mention his skills in combat. Particularly after the gun battle in Taylor's house and the skirmish in Amphionides's office. Yeah, Bolan had revealed himself in some ways, and Helonas would attempt to use that knowledge to his advantage.

"Did you catch all of that, Jack?" Bolan asked as he trotted down the hall.

"Just your side of it, Sarge," Jack's voice crackled back. "What's up?"

"Seventeen November split, and they took Hyde-Baker with them. I'm going to have to find them."

"I don't know, buddy," Grimaldi retorted with skepticism in his tone. "Athens is a mighty big place, not to mention the Greek countryside. They could be anywhere."

"I think I know how to narrow that search by a good margin," Bolan replied as he opened the door to the sedan and got behind the wheel.

"How's that?"

As Bolan started the engine he said, "Get me directions to the offices of the Pontiki newspaper."

THE EXECUTIONER pushed through the doors of the political newspaper and walked to the front desk. His purpose here was simple. He wanted information and he knew he'd come to the right place. The man called Midas probably didn't know about his uncle yet, or the fact that their plans to assassinate Albertson had failed. According to the information he'd gleaned from Taylor, Midas was nothing more than a worm anyway. Amphionides had used the guy as a means to accomplish an end.

Once Midas knew the truth, there was very little chance his

resistance would hold. Bolan was counting on that and he meant to use every means at his disposal to extract the information he wanted.

"I'm looking for Midas," he told the receptionist. "Is he in?"

The woman behind the desk smiled sensually at the tall, dark-haired and blue-eyed man. Bolan was used to the reaction. Women seemed to be attracted to his ruggedness.

"No, sir, I'm afraid he is not. May I ask the nature of your visit?"

"I have some information for him that he requested," he said. Bolan smiled his best charm smile and added, "I'm a regular source."

She nodded in understanding. "I see. You speak English like an American."

"I am an American," he said. "I live and work here on business."

"Well, in that case perhaps we could get together some time," she said. The woman was actually very attractive. Long legs peeked out from her desk, and dark hair cascaded down her back. Luminous eyes flashed at Bolan, and he had to admit the woman was a looker. It was too bad he'd never call her. What he needed right now was a location.

"Maybe we could," he told her. "May I have your number?"

"Sure." She whipped out a pen and notepad, scribbled the information and ripped off the sheet, handing it to Bolan with another dazzling grin.

"Thanks. I'll call you soon."

"And as far as Midas's concerned," she continued, "you'll probably find him at the Nicropolahdis pub."

"Where is it?" he said.

She jerked her thumb in the general direction and replied, "Two blocks down."

He saluted her with the piece of paper and said, "Thanks, doll."

"Anytime."

The Executioner was glad to get out of there, and he could

hear Grimaldi snickering in his ear. That was quite all right, given the fact the Stony Man pilot had a reputation around the Farm as quite a ladies' man.

"What are you laughing about?" Bolan said through a grin.

"You sounded like some love-burned high-school kid, Sarge," Grimaldi said. He tried to mimic the Executioner's pinched, New England accent and said, "Maybe we could. May I have your number? Thanks. I'll call you soon."

Then Grimaldi couldn't contain himself any more and began to guffaw in Bolan's ear. The Executioner couldn't help but smile at his friend. And it was pretty damn funny, the pilot's imitation and all. Nonetheless, they still had business to conduct, although the soldier wasn't ungrateful for a bit of comic relief.

"Don't quit your day job, Jack. I'm sure Vegas isn't looking to have you back."

People cast some weird glances at Bolan as he passed them, probably wondering why in the hell this guy was talking to himself. The Executioner ignored them, choosing to concentrate on the task at hand. He found the pub and entered through the doors, nearly choking on the heavy scent of cigarette smoke and stale liquor.

As the room came into focus, Bolan studied the interior. It was getting close to lunchtime, but the place hadn't really seen the noon-time rush yet. If there even were such a thing in Athens. A bar shaped like a half moon took up the center of the pub. There was a grill on the other half where a chef and barmaid worked. On the outside walls there were booths and tables. The place was dimly lit, and some sort of Greek music was playing through the wall-mounted speakers.

It took a moment or two for Bolan's eyes to adjust, but he quickly spotted Midas seated in a corner. The guy was engaged in a conversation with a woman, his back to the door, so he didn't see the Executioner enter. Bolan sauntered over to the table, attempting to look as casual as he could so as not to alarm the occupants. He stopped in front of the table, and Midas quit talking long enough to look at the new arrival.

Something bordering on surprise mixed with fear splashed across Midas's dark features, and he started to bring his hands beneath the table. Bolan reached into his jacket as he sat down in next to the woman, forcing her over against the wall of the booth. He brought the pistol up under the table and favored Midas with a warning smile.

"Uh-uh, pal," Bolan counseled him. "Don't think about doing anything stupid. Keep your hands on the table. I just want to chat."

"What do you want, Michalis?"

"Come on, Midas, we both know that's not who I really am, so quit playing stupid to save your own skin. Amphionides is dead, and so is the assassin he hired to kill the conference witness. It's over."

"And you're here to kill me now?"

Bolan shook his head. "Not at all. You're no threat to anybody, Midas. You're a weakling and a coward, and you stand to inherit millions from Amphionides's estate. That is, of course, unless the Greek cabinet decides to confiscate that money as an appropriation for all of the trouble he caused. You could be on your way to the poor house."

"What do you want from me?"

"I want to know where Helonas ran off to," Bolan growled. "I have some unfinished business with him."

"What makes you think I know that?" Midas replied coolly.

"I'm not stupid," Bolan said. "I know about your involvement with 17 November, and about the money you were stashing away. Money that Helonas was giving you. Remember that it was you who helped to set up the meet between us. I also think you're the one who told Amphionides we were going to Portsmouth."

"Why would I turn in my own cousin?" Midas challenged Bolan.

"Who cares?" the Executioner ventured. "You competed with Helonas for the attention of Amphionides, and you hated the fact that he was making a difference. Maybe you figured to head up 17 November with him out of the way. It would appear your plan backfired."

"That is quite a story," Midas retorted, raising one eyebrow and smiling wanly. "You have a vivid imagination."

"I also have very little time left," Bolan said, jabbing the gun into Midas's gut to remind the reporter he was running out of patience. "So tell me where to find Helonas."

"I will not."

"Then you're a dead man."

"Wait...let me reconsider."

"You had best hurry, Midas."

"It is probable that 17 November would split up if they had been discovered. I don't think they would stay together, which means that Cyril and the other members of the group could be scattered all throughout Athens. They might be anywhere."

"No dice," Bolan shot back. "They took Hyde-Baker with them. They obviously believe they still have leverage as long as she's a prisoner. Where would they take her?"

"There is only one place I can think of in that case," Midas said quickly. "They probably retreated to their base on Sikinos."

"Where's that?"

"An island south of Greece. It is very small and not heavily populated. There is an isle off its coast to the southwest, considered to be part of Sikinos, and that's where the base is. Nobody but the members know it is there."

"Already working up the specs on it, Sarge," Grimaldi's voice said through the earpiece.

"Fine," Bolan said. He tucked his pistol into his jacket as he rose, turned to leave and then said on afterthought, "Don't bother trying to warn them, Midas. You're under surveillance as we speak, and any transmissions to that island will be monitored. As a matter of fact, I'd walk lightly from here on out. I'm sure the authorities will be looking for any reason to lock you away for good."

Midas only nodded, glaring with hatred at the Executioner.

Bolan didn't let it affect him. It would give Midas something to think about. Perhaps he'd clean up his act.

The soldier left the pub and spoke softly into his microphone as he headed for the newspaper office where he'd left the sedan. "Jack, meet me at the airport. It's time to conclude our business with 17 November."

Sikinos Isle, Aegean Sea

Mack Bolan studied the water rippling out below him in the whirlwind of the chopper blades. The Bell Model 206A Jet-Ranger Grimaldi had rented from a tour company hovered about ten yards above the blue-green sea.

Bolan had acquired equipment from Taylor's contacts within Greece. He was attired in the form-fitting blacksuit he'd brought with him, Taylor and Godforth having retrieved his bag from her house in Athens.

He had his Beretta inside a waterproof backpack; the weapon was now cleaned and loaded with a fresh clip. A military canvas belt encircled his waist, with various pouches containing spare magazines for the Beretta and .44 Magnum Desert Eagle. The huge Israeli-made pistol was in the bag, as well.

Bolan was also carrying a newly acquired addition to his arsenal, and one that was becoming very popular with the Executioner because of its versatility and quality. It was a Belgium-made FNC, the carbine version of the FAL designed by Fabrique Nationale. The assault rifle fired 5.56 mm NATO ammunition from a 30-round box magazine, and it had a cyclic rate of about 700 rounds per minute. The most notable features of the weapon—and the reasons it was most popular with the soldier—were its ease of handling and design for prolonged use in harsh conditions.

The bag contained a few other goodies. Bolan liked to be prepared, especially when he didn't know what he might be facing. The bag also held grenades, a grappling hook, fifty feet of rope and a couple of sticks of C-4 plastique, along with primers and an electronic detonator.

The Executioner was prepared to do final battle with 17 November—and it was a battle from which he knew only one victor could emerge.

"I'm out, Jack," Bolan said.

"Good luck, Sarge," Grimaldi replied through the earpiece. "Call me when you're ready for pickup."

Bolan grumbled a reply and then bailed from the JetRanger. He wished he had the support of Grimaldi going into the situation, but there was no practical way for them to get a military helicopter, equipped with the proper munitions for air support, without contacting Stony Man to pull some strings. There just wasn't enough time, and Bolan was concerned that every minute that passed was one closer to the end of Hyde-Baker's life.

The Executioner hit the chilling waters of the Aegean and began to swim for the shore. While it was rather warm that afternoon, the icy spray sent a shiver through Bolan's body. He began to pump his arm and leg muscles to propel himself through the water and he was on shore within a minute.

Bolan retrieved the Beretta and Desert Eagle, holstering the weapons in their respective places, and then pulled some additional materials from the bag. Through the SAS, Taylor had managed to secure some British versions of the U.S. M-26 fragmentation grenade. The soldier secured the four HE grenades to his webbing and then set off through the vegetation.

The foliage was thick and green through many parts of the small island. Natives had it this small chunk of land—just a speck on the map—was deserted. The isle was actually owned by the Greek government, and it was considered open land for anyone to look at it. Nobody was actually allowed to set up residence on such protected lands, but that wouldn't make any difference to 17 November.

Midas had said there was a base of operations here; that meant considerable work had been done to secure the place. Bolan surmised it was possible he would actually face some significant security measures, and he mentally prepared himself for any nasty surprises that might await him. For some strange reason, the Executioner realized he was walking into a possible trap, yet he was going anyway. Most would have considered that insane—he considered it duty.

Bolan moved effortlessly and quietly through the thick vegetation. Trees spread out above him, birds called ceaselessly and steam rose from the ground. The salty breezes of the Aegean blew through the trees, tickling Bolan's nostrils as he pressed onward. The isle had approximately a three-mile diameter, so he knew it wouldn't take him long to do his reconnaissance. If 17 November were there, he'd find them soon enough.

Almost as if on cue, Bolan passed a high stand of trees that went upward and suddenly met with a clearing. Approximately one hundred yards ahead he got his first glimpse of 17 November's handiwork. The house was built from brick and measured about thirty yards wide by twenty deep. It was two stories, and a small balcony enclosed by wrought iron spanned the entire rear of the second floor. Large brick pillars were placed at almost strategic points along that, and the Executioner could barely see something on them.

Bolan squinted, but he still couldn't see what the holes were. He finally remembered the FNC and how the weapon had been equipped with a 10-power scope. The soldier pulled the FNC from the bag and aimed it at one of the posts, dropping the caps from the scope and studying the house up close.

The holes were firing ports! The terrorists had literally designed the house to be defended like some fortress, which meant there were probably other features the Executioner couldn't see. He traversed downward with the barrel and studied the first floor. The windows looked as if they were reinforced, possibly bulletproof glass, and that wasn't just normal brick siding. There was quality in the work there.

Bolan lowered the FNC, snatching a special clip from his belt and trading it with the normal one. The magazine he inserted had a 10-round capacity, but the tips were soft-nosed and contained liquid Teflon. The weight of slugs in most 5.56 mm ammunition had a tendency to drop considerably over distance or suffer deflection from heat expansion—it was a trade off with lower-caliber high-velocity ammunition. In this instance, 5.56 mm wasn't exactly the best for sniping purposes. The lighter-weight bullets he used, however, would do the trick nicely and prevented having to tote an additional piece of hardware.

Bolan chambered the first round and then raised the scope to his eye. He could make out four sentries—two up and two down—on that side of the house. The lower guards didn't have any real cover and no firing positions behind brick pillars, so he decided to take out the upper pair first. He set his sights on one, adjusted slightly and then took a deep breath and let half out.

The Executioner's finger grazed the trigger with a single, fluid motion.

The liquid-Teflon round punched through the guy's skull, splitting it down the middle before it burst out the other side. The pressure of the bullet blew out his left eyeball even as he collapsed to the ground.

Bolan swung the muzzle into acquisition of the second guy, who had frozen one moment to watch his comrade fall. The surprised sentry turned to run for cover but didn't make it. The Executioner's shot caught him through the neck, severing the carotid artery and shattering the larynx. The guy was gargling blood before he fell, the ghastly sight visible through the scope.

Bolan swung the weapon toward ground level while thumbing the selector switch to 3-round burst capacity. He sighted on one of the terrorists who was running for the corner of the house, led him slightly and then depressed the trigger. The first round missed but the other two caught the sentry in the thigh and shoulder. He collapsed into a roll and Bolan lurched from his cover on the edge of the tree line.

The fourth sentry was faced in his general direction, but Bolan had gained about half the distance to the house before the guy saw him. At that point it was too late. As the sentry brought his weapon to bear, Bolan dropped to one knee, raised the FNC to his shoulder and fired, directing the muzzle in a rising burst. All three of the special 5.56 mm rounds drilled through the terrorist's torso in a pattern, striking pelvis, belly and chest. The gunman flopped onto his back and coughed his last breath.

Bolan dropped the clip and slammed the fresh 30-round box home on the move.

He reached the edge of the house, sending a mercy round into the terrorist writhing on the ground from the shots he'd taken in the arm and leg. The Executioner moved to the edge, crouched and peered around the corner. There was no movement and no sign of further resistance. He lurched from his cover and made for the front of the brick stronghold.

THE SOUND OF GUNFIRE above told Cyril Helonas and the others that the moment had come.

The enemy was storming their island refuge, and Helonas was as anxious to face his father's murderer as the rest of 17 November. All of their plans for this day had failed, and it was Belasko who was behind it. How one man could have ever sent mayhem through the ranks of their organization was beyond Helonas's comprehension. But it really didn't matter now.

All that mattered was the death of this demon; Cyril Helonas meant to see this through to that end.

Jason, Mette and eight others from the group were gathered in the basement, ready to bring the fight to their sworn opponent. Helonas had counseled them in the plans to lead Belasko like the lamb to the slaughter. They were to stage their ambush at key points throughout the house in pairs, increasing the pressure exponentially until Belasko had the entire team on him.

Then it would be too late and he would die under a merciless onslaught of firepower such as no traitor like him had ever seen before.

"Let us pray the gods go with us," Helonas told them. They offered up a moment of silence and then split into their individual teams.

Helonas had Jason and Mette with him, and they would be the last group to confront Bolan. If all else failed—and Helonas had already considered the possibility—there was the option to destroy the house. It might mean self-sacrifice, but the terrorists were prepared for it if it meant the preservation of 17 November. Surely someone would carry on in their stead.

They had to make their stand now, and there was no turning back.

The group ascended the stairs in their two-person teams, armed with various makes of machine pistols, handguns and assault rifles. As they reached the ground floor, some secured themselves behind assigned doorways or in darkened rooms, while others continued to the second floor. A walkway encircled the main room, branching off the stairs that led to the upper story off the front door.

There was only one entrance in or out, and the teams set up to take Belasko as soon as he came through it. There was an entrance on the second floor in the rear—the one off the balcony—but that would be an impractical route. After all, it wasn't like Belasko could climb walls.

Helonas waited in the shadows of an alcove off the large adjoining kitchen and counted the seconds. With each passing moment his heart beat faster until he thought it was going to burst with the anticipation. The Greek terrorist could almost taste the bittersweet revenge in his mouth, as if he were anticipating a favorite dish not served to him since childhood.

When Belasko came through that door, he would be a dead man.

MACK BOLAN KNEW that going through the front door would be suicide.

Helonas had surely prepared for the Executioner's arrival, and the warrior's sixth sense warned him of impending doom if he came through the main entrance like gangbusters. His advancement to this point had been just a little too easy to suit his tastes, and that spelled trouble in Bolan's mind. There was only one other way to deal with this problem.

He'd have to access it on his own terms.

Bolan moved back from the corner of the house and backtracked to the balcony on the rear. He'd remembered a single door built into the wall on the second floor, and that seemed like his best bet. A stick of C-4 against the door would do nicely, and the addition of grenades could clear the room of any potential resistance.

The Executioner slung the FNC under his arm and then produced the rope and grappling hook. He heaved the metal claw up to the second floor, and tines of tempered steel wrapped around one of the pillars before biting into the brick facade. Bolan tested the rope with his weight and then vaulted up it like a spider. He climbed hand over hand and emerged on the second floor within eight seconds.

Moving to the door, Bolan slapped a one-pound stick of C-4 on the side of the hinges and planted the fuse. He crossed to one end of the balcony, ducked low and flipped the switch on the detonator. Half of the stick would have been more than enough to effectively clear the door, but Bolan was betting on internal reinforcement, while also doubling up for a psychological effect.

The whoosh of flaming wood, metal and brick was overpowering in the countrylike silence of the area. The explosion rang in Bolan's ears as the door completely separated from its hinges and flew inward, taking chunks of sharp steel and glass with it. The brick around the area of the C-4 completely shattered to rock dust under the force of the plastic explosive.

Bolan charged through the room, FNC up and ready for resistance. He didn't encounter any, and the Executioner moved through the wide room and toward an inner door. The room itself took up that entire side of the house. It was filled with bunks arranged side by side in neat order. He continued onward through the inner door and emerged into a hallway filled with surprised terrorists.

Two were standing practically next to him and had their weapons raised, although they weren't pointed in his direction. There was a lot of shouting and confusion, which indicated Bolan had rendered the surprise he'd hoped for.

The pair closest to him tried to swing their muzzles into range, but Bolan shot them with a burst of lead. One of the gunners toppled forward, his chest exploding under the impact of high-velocity rounds at close range. The other member was a woman. The autofire from the FNC drove her backward and over the railing, and her corpse plunged to the ground floor.

Two more terrorists rushed toward him on the left, while another pair directly across from him—positioned on the far balcony—began to fire their machine pistols. Another pair revealed themselves from below and tried to move into a better vantage point so they could lay down their own field of fire.

The Executioner hit the floor, deciding to deal with the two closest terrorists first. He triggered his FNC, nearly emptying the magazine on them in a fusillade of 5.56 mm rounds. The bullets blew holes in their upper torsos and punctured vital organs, shredding flesh with merciless accuracy. The two terrorists practically fell on each other, crumpling to the ground under Bolan's heavy assault.

The Executioner rolled away from the autofire being poured into the wall immediately above him. He retrieved one of the grenades as he rolled, popping the pin with his thumb and hurling it across the gap in an overhand toss. Before it exploded on the other side, Bolan lobbed a second HE bomb over the railing. The two explosions were only seconds apart, threatening to shake the building to its foundations in the echo of the blasts. The screams of agony coming from the opposing balcony and the floor below told him the grenades had produced the desired results.

Bolan jumped to his feet and saw the charred remains of one terrorist hanging over the edge of the railing. Flames had incinerated a good portion of the couch below, and now they were licking at other objects. The fire was already climbing the curtain and hot embers even ignited a throw rug. It wouldn't be long before the whole place went up.

Bolan saw one of the terrorists below had managed to escape the better part of the blast. The guy was bleeding from multiple shrapnel wounds, but he was standing and raging mad. He screamed at Bolan as the Executioner sprinted around the balcony and headed toward the stairs. The guy raised his Zastava M-85 SMG and began to fire on the soldier's position.

The soldier went low, diving to the stairs and bringing the FNC to bear. He triggered the weapon and got two shots off before the bolt locked back. He rolled over to avoid a fresh burst of fire from the Zastava, drawing his Beretta 93-R from its holster. He selected 3-round bursts and completed one roll before taking careful aim and firing. The 9 mm Parabellum rounds crashed through the terrorist's stomach, ripping out part of his liver and spleen before he dropped his SMG and fell to the ground dead.

The curtains and rug were now fully engulfed, flames licking at any source of fuel that would continue to feed it. Dark smoke was beginning to belch from the combustibles as they were consumed by fire. Bolan got to his feet and continued down the steps.

He reached the first floor and was about to exit the house when Jason and Mette burst from separate hiding places and began to fire on him. One of the rounds from Jason's pistol ripped through the taut skin drawn over the Executioner's left ribs. Bolan went to one knee, deciding to take Jason first. He squeezed the trigger of the Beretta, letting the weapon cycle through all three shots.

Jason dived away in time, the trio of rounds missing him by mere inches. Bolan whirled to see Mette closing in, his pistol raised, but he wasn't firing. The Executioner had his own pistol up and pointed directly at a point where Mette's heart was.

"Kill him, you dumb shit!" Jason was yelling.

Bolan could see Mette's fingers whiten as he gripped the pistol, his hand beginning to shake, but there was something hesitant in the young man's eyes. It suddenly occurred to Bolan that Mette had never killed anyone before. He was just too young, and he'd probably only joined 17 November because Jason had.

The Executioner looked behind him in time to see Jason rise and raise his pistol. The sound of a single gunshot echoed through the open house, but it wasn't Bolan who felt the bullet pierce his flesh. Jason flinched slightly and then looked down at his stomach in surprise. A red stain was rapidly spreading across his shirt. He looked up at the Executioner a moment before the light faded from his eyes and then landed on the cold, unyielding wooden floor in a heap.

Bolan looked back at Mette in surprise.

The kid still had his pistol raised—muzzle smoking from the single shot—and he was simply staring blankly ahead. He didn't meet the Executioner's gaze for some time. Bolan finally stood and slowly approached the young man, lowering his own pistol and putting his hand out. Mette remained motionless, just staring into space as if he were in some sort of trance.

"Give me the gun, Mette," Bolan said quietly. "You can still walk away from this. You can still have a normal life."

The kid finally looked at the Executioner as tears began to well up in his eyes. "I never really believed in this, you know?"

Bolan nodded. "I know."

Mette handed the pistol to him, and Bolan urged the youth to accompany him. The smoke was becoming unbearable, and the soldier could begin to taste and smell the pungent odors as the toxic gases increased. Most of it was rising toward the high ceiling, but it was quickly making its way across that expanse and down the sides.

Bolan almost had Mette to the front door when he stopped in his tracks at the sound of scraping noise, barely audible above the crackle of the flames. Bolan reached up to his webbing and secured a grenade with his left hand as he holstered the Beretta with his right.

"How touching!" a voice called behind them.

Bolan and Mette turned slowly.

The Executioner didn't have to see the speaker—he knew the voice. He'd heard its deep, melodic tones many times before, although never with the scorn that he heard in it now.

Cyril Helonas stood ten yards from them, an AKSU-74 clutched in his hands.

"You have destroyed everything that we worked so hard to preserve, Belasko."

"Tough," Bolan said.

Helonas obviously hadn't noticed the HE grenade Bolan had palmed. It would have been difficult to see from the distance, given the poor lighting, the smoke and the building heat. Not to mention the fact Bolan had the back of his hand facing Helonas. The Greek terror-monger had only really looked for guns, and anything less he'd dismissed out of hand.

"For the death of my father," Helonas said, apparently unaffected by Bolan's cynicism, "and for your crimes against 17 November, I commit you to hell."

You first, the Executioner thought.

Bolan let the spoon go from the grenade and counted two seconds before tossing it. Helonas had obviously been expecting a more direct attack, and the sight of the grenade flying in his direction took the terrorist off guard. Bolan used the advantage to open the door and haul Mette out with him. He threw the kid down behind the cover of the brick exterior.

There was a shout of surprise from Helonas that was cut off by the ignition of the high-explosive grenade. Shrapnel and intense heat ripped through the terrorist's body, the concussion breaking bones in his chest and literally separating his head from his neck. The decapitated, shredded corpse crumpled to the ground in a heap, and the fire grabbed hungrily at his clothing.

Bolan hauled Mette to his feet and brought him into the doorway to stare at the remains of Helonas.

"You made the right choice," the Executioner told him.

Epilogue

Athens, Greece

Nobody recognized the tall, distinguished gentleman with the mop of red hair, along with the thick sideburns, mustache and beard to match. He was tall, somber looking, with green eyes and a dark complexion. He wore a conservative tweed suit that was tailored to his lean physique. He also had press credentials that allowed him inside the meeting room, a privilege that had obviously been reserved for very few.

And it was just as well.

Mack Bolan had attracted enough attention over the past few days that to show his face anymore would have begun to elicit some very uncomfortable questions—questions he would rather have avoided.

He wished for the opportunity to say goodbye to Taylor and Godforth, but his business didn't allow for long-term relationships. It was a part of the job that Bolan had come to accept long ago. He wasn't too far from where they stood, but they didn't recognize him. They had arranged this pretty corny disguise through Stony Man's contacts, and Bolan would be much happier the sooner he could escape the crazy get-up.

But for the time being, it was necessary.

The conference had been postponed for a few days in light of the incident involving Amphionides and other sympathizers in the Greek cabinet. Those corrupt members had been removed immediately from their appointments, and it looked as if the future might hold better things for the people of Greece.

Mette had helped Bolan retrieve Undersecretary Audrey Hyde-Baker from a toolshed where they'd hidden her on the grounds near the house. The British diplomat now sat with the committee, despite her weakened state, and Bolan had to admit he admired this gutsy woman. She'd endured considerable trauma at the hands of Helonas and 17 November, and she'd come out the other side no lesser for it.

"Mr. Albertson," she spoke up, addressing the ex-CIA spook as he sat in the lone chair, "tell us your position and reason for appearing before this panel."

"I am the former CIA section chief for the Balkan-states, and I am here to disclose the identities of sympathizers within the Greek government toward known terrorist organizations."

"And is there any specific organization to which you are referring?"

"Yes, Madam Secretary."

"Would you care to disclose the name of this organization?"

"There were sympathizers within the Greek government who had either direct or indirect affiliation with the terrorist organization 17 November."

"It is the understanding of this panel that those affiliate members have been identified and removed from their positions," Hyde-Baker replied. "You have seen the list of those members. Is it your testimony that all affiliate members have been positively identified?"

"Yes, ma'am."

"And is it also your belief that 17 November was responsible for the death of Brigadier Stephen Saunders, the British attaché to this country?"

"I know it for a fact."

"And do you know the name of the individual responsible for the death of Brigadier Saunders?"

"No, I do not," Albertson replied quickly. "However, it was no secret that 17 November claimed responsibility for the act, and that the assassination did keep within the parameters of 17 November's methods of operating."

"And how did you come by this information?" the justice minister asked.

"It was part of the intelligence we'd collected on terrorist operations within Greece."

A ripple of astonishment went through everyone in the room with the exception of Bolan. It didn't surprise him to hear this new bit of information, particularly not from a former member of the CIA. It was as he'd believed from the beginning—there was no substitute for decisive action. Terrorists didn't understand anything but swift and direct consequences in response to their actions.

Bolan had delivered those consequences, and for the time being 17 November wouldn't be a threat to anyone. That thought brought just a glimmer of hope and satisfaction to the Executioner's spirit. Yeah, it made it all worthwhile to watch Albertson and the governments represented here work together to find better solutions for battling worldwide terrorism.

And Mack Bolan looked on.